I couldn't have felt more sorry for her. After all, I read more than my fair share of books that make me keep the light on all night long. And lots of books that make me sad, or anxious, till things work out right. But I don't end up in a state like her, halfway to fainting because of three or four grisly pages, and not even able to look at the cover of that book again without wanting to shudder.

'A gift', her mother called it. But, the more Imogen told me about it, the more I thought that that was totally the wrong word.

'Curse' was more like it.

Yes. Not 'gift', but 'curse'. . .

ANNE FINE

Bad Dreams

Illustrated by Susan Winter

CORGI YEARLING BOOKS

BAD DREAMS
A CORGI YEARLING BOOK 9780440868095

First published in Great Britain by Doubleday,
an imprint of Random House Children's Books

Doubleday edition published 2000
Corgi Yearling edition published 2001
This edition published 2006

3 5 7 9 10 8 6 4

Corgi Yearling Books are published by Transworld Publishers,
61–63 Uxbridge Road, London W5 5SA,
a division of The Random House Group Ltd.

Addresses for Random House Group Ltd companies outside the UK
can be found at: www.randomhouse.co.uk

THE RANDOM HOUSE GROUP Limited Reg. No. 954009
www.kidsatrandomhouse.co.uk

The Random House Group Limited makes every effort to ensure that the
papers used in its books are made from trees that have been legally
sourced from well-managed and credibly certified forests. Our paper
procurement policy can be found at: www.randomhouse.co.uk/paper.htm.

Mixed Sources
Product group from well-managed
forests and other controlled sources
www.fsc.org Cert no. TT-COC-2139
© 1996 Forest Stewardship Council
FSC

A CIP catalogue record for this book is available from
the British Library.

Printed and bound in Great Britain by
Cox & Wyman Ltd, Reading, Berkshire

For Jon Appleton,
without whom . . .

CHAPTER ONE

It's only been bothering me a tiny bit. But still, Mr Hooper saw my uneasy look.

'What ho, Mel!' he offered. 'A trouble shared is a trouble halved?'

I shook my head. 'No, thanks. It's too private.'

'Write it down, then,' he told me. 'If something's gnawing at you, shove it on paper.'

I waved at the books round us, shelf upon shelf of them, up to the ceiling.

'Is that what the writers of some of these were doing?'

'Quite a few, I should think,' he said. 'False

names, true stories, and they make a mint. You try it. I'll buy a copy.'

He went off chuckling and I sat down to think. Why not? I'm good at stories. I could call it *Bad Dreams*. Or even, *Imogen Imagines*, since it would be about her, and how she came to our school and spooked all of us – especially me – with her weirdness, and all of her horrible imaginings.

This is how it started. She turned up halfway through one morning in summer term. She came through the doorway behind Mrs Trent, who simply handed her over and left in a hurry.

Mr Hooper had only the briefest of chats with her at the desk before turning to the rest of us. 'Class, this is Imogen Tate, who's joining us from another school.'

She looked embarrassed, and we stared. She was already dressed in our boring old school uniform, with her hair in plain bunches. There was absolutely nothing special about her, but in spite of that everyone wanted to be her first-week minder. Almost all of them put their hands up.

But Mr Hooper said, 'And I pick – Melanie!'

I was astonished. '*Me?*'

'Well,' he said, 'why not?'

'I didn't put my hand up.'

'That doesn't matter,' he said. 'It'll be nice for

you to have someone in that empty seat.'

I didn't think so, but I couldn't say. Maybe I should explain. I'm the class bookworm. I don't mix much with the others because I like reading better. All the way up the school it's bothered my teachers. One after another, they've tried to prise the books out of my hands, and get me to join in more.

Yet I still prefer reading.

But you can't be rude to someone who's new, and standing there trembling. So I just patted the spare chair at my side, and she came over. And as she was busy unpacking her pens and pencils into the desk, I finally thought of something friendly to say.

'I like that necklace you're wearing. Is it gold?'
She nodded shyly.

'*Real* gold?'

'Yes,' she said. 'My granny gave it to my mother, and now it's been passed down to me.'

I peered at it more closely. It had strange little scratchy markings, and looked fine and slinky enough to be spilled into a teaspoon.

'You're so lucky,' I told her, still trying to be nice. 'I'm sure no-one will ever pass anything special down to me.'

As if I'd suddenly reminded her of something, she stopped in the middle of her unpacking and gave me a look. 'Then maybe you're the lucky one,' she told me.

I stared at her. 'What do you mean?'

She wouldn't say. In fact, she hardly said anything at all after that, except things like, 'Should I write this in the red book?' and, 'Do I use pen or pencil to do this?' and, 'Can I borrow your ruler?'

I bet she didn't even realize that what she'd said stuck in my mind. But it was like the first clue in a book. It just stuck out. And it was *strange*.

CHAPTER TWO

She was no good at schoolwork. You could tell Mr Hooper was amazed how badly she did in all the tests he set her. But he still made her book monitor, along with me.

'Since Melly's looking after you,' he explained.

'Must I?' she asked him. 'I hate books.'

I was astonished. 'Hate them? Actually *hate* them?'

She blushed. 'Well,' she said, 'I just don't get on with them very well.'

What can you say? I love books more than anything. Left to myself, I wouldn't come to school at all. I'd spend my whole life reading. 'Go out,' my mother tells me. 'It's lovely today. Go and play in the fresh air.' But I'd rather stay in my bedroom, and read about other children going out to play.

'You're not a bit like me, then,' I told Imogen. 'You know those battered old Christmas albums you see in jumble sales that have a picture on the front of a girl reading another album just the same, with a picture of herself on the cover? You know how they go on, down and down, smaller and smaller, like boxes inside boxes, until the girl's too small to be seen?'

'Yes, I've seen those.'

'Well,' I said, 'that's who I want to be. That girl who's reading all the other lives in from the outside.'

Now it was her turn to look at me as if I were loopy. 'Really?'

'Yes,' I admitted. 'That's who I'd like to be more than anyone in the world.'

And then I showed her how to use the card index in the book corner. And how to stamp the books out, and how to tell from the coloured sticker on the spine whether it should go back in Older Readers, or Poetry, or Project Work.

She had a funny way of picking up the books – gingerly, as if they might scorch her. After a few minutes, I asked her, as a joke:

'Didn't you have any of these in your old school?'

She made a face. 'Oh, yes,' she said. 'We had them. It's just that I hardly ever had to go near them.'

Strange thing to say. And I was just thinking, 'No wonder her work's so bad', when, suddenly, I saw her jump.

'Oh!' she said, startled.

'What's the matter?'

'Nothing.'

But I couldn't help noticing she hadn't touched that book again. She was staring at it nervously.

'It's that book, isn't it?' I said. 'Something about it has upset you.'

'Don't be silly,' she said. But she had definitely gone red again.

I'm not an idiot. I kept a watch. And only a few minutes later, I saw it happen a second time. Imogen picked up a different book, and dropped it as if it had stung her.

As if it were red hot.

'What's up?' I asked again.

'Nothing.'

I think, when people try to fool you, they can practically expect you to start spying on them. And that's why I was watching so closely when, later that morning, Mr Hooper hurried past her without a single word, then, noticing her anxious little 'new-girl' face, stopped guiltily and thrust the book he happened to be carrying into her hand.

'Here, Imogen,' he said. 'You say you don't like books. Try this one – *Violet's Game*. Melly says it's brilliant. It's about a girl called Violet. That's her you can see on the cover, cuddling that kitten. And she—'

He broke off because Imogen was already backing away. 'Oh, no! I couldn't bear it! I can't stand stories about animals that have been hurt.'

Mr Hooper looked a bit surprised. 'Sorry,' he said. 'I hadn't realized you'd already read it.'

'Oh, no.' Imogen started to shake her head, then stopped, embarrassed. And Mr Hooper looked a little embarrassed, too. After all, just because *Violet's Game* has only just come into our class book corner, it didn't mean Imogen couldn't have come across it back in her old school.

'Well, at least it ends happily,' Mr Hooper reminded her. Then the bell rang, and he rushed off to get his coffee.

So I was the only one left to see Imogen running her finger gently over the kitten in the picture on the cover, and muttering, 'Good!'

As if she were glad to hear it.

And as if it were news.

Chapter Three

Was she more careful after that? I couldn't say. If you don't know exactly what you're looking for, you're often not sure what you've seen. She acted normally enough from then on. I heard her draw her breath in sharply once or twice. But the top shelf is pretty high, and it can be tiring, reaching up over and over to put things back after wet break.

But I was still curious about her and books. So whenever I came across one I really loved, I held it up.

'Have you read this?'

Sometimes she nodded. Sometimes she shook

her head. But she never burst out with the sort of thing everyone else says.

'Oh yes! Didn't you just *love* the bit where his head flipped off, and it turned out he was an alien?'

Or, 'I *hated* the creepy old lady. I knew she was out to get them from the very first page.'

Or even things like, 'Did you cry when the dog died? I cried *buckets*. My dad had to make me a cup of tea!'

No, she'd just put on that closed look people get when they're trying to get past charity collectors in the street. She'd try to fob me off.

'I think I read it, yes.'

'You must *remember*.'

She'd try and distract me. Even though hardly anyone had come near the book corner for days, she'd pretend we were so busy she had to interrupt to ask, 'Should this book here be put away? Or do I leave it out for the next project group?'

And I'd give up.

But, next day, when I held one of my favourites up to her face, I did quite definitely see her shudder.

'You have read this one, then? You know what it's about.'

'Well, *sort* of . . .'

'Didn't you get to finish it?'

19

She tossed her head vaguely. You couldn't tell if she meant yes, or no.

'Well, *did* you?'

She wouldn't answer. She just asked a question of her own. 'What did you want to say about it, anyway?'

'Nothing,' I muttered grumpily, and went back to my sorting. I had decided there was no point in trying to talk to Imogen about the books. I think, if two of you have read the same things, you should be able to have a good long chat about them, not have to put up with the other person ending each conversation by staring uncomfortably at her feet, and mumbling things like, 'Yes, I suppose so,' or, 'I'm not sure I remember that bit very well,' or, 'Maybe that wasn't actually the book I read.' I felt so cross about it, I even complained about her to Mr Hooper.

'Why have you dumped her on me? She's not much of a reader.'

He burst out laughing. 'Melly, compared with you, no-one in this class is a reader.'

I shook my head. 'No,' I said stubbornly. 'There's more to it than that. She says she's read things when she really hasn't.'

'Maybe you intimidate her,' he said. And then he added firmly, 'Just make an effort to be friendly, Mel. A week's not long. It won't hurt you.'

Seeing my face, he reached behind him to the

20

shelf, and tipped a big fat book out of a jiffy bag into my hands.

'There you are, Mel,' he said. 'Here's a reward for all your sufferings. And don't expect to be able to talk to Imogen about this one, because practically nobody else in the world has read it.'

'How do you know?'

'Because it's hot off the press,' he said proudly. 'A free gift from the publishers for ordering all those other books at the end of last term.'

I turned it over. *Red Rock*, by Alston Byers. The cover was a bit soppy. A little girl in a blue frock was picking up stones. But some of the best books in the world have the worst covers, so I started it anyway, under the desk at the end of Maths Workbook.

It was amazing. I thought at first it was going to be one of those stories too stuffed with descriptions. It seemed to start with an awful lot of heat hazes lying over scrubland, and people leaning against the doors of sun-blistered shacks.

But suddenly it turned into a real nail-biter about a tribe of Indians who got fed up with tourists chipping off bits of their famous sacred red rock, to take home as souvenirs. So they put a curse on all the bits missing. Instantly, all over the world, reports started coming in of horrible deaths, and gruesome accidents, and weird diseases, as if some ghastly jump-in-your-seat horror video was playing everywhere, but, this time, for real.

I couldn't put the book down. Mr Hooper went through all his usual routines.

'Am I going to have to take that book off you till going home time, Melly?'

'I hope you're not rushing that written work to get back to your reading.'

'What's all this Mrs Springer tells me about you hiding that book I gave you under your song sheet?'

But it was impossible to stop reading. By this time in the story, people couldn't post back their bits of red rock fast enough. But one little girl, the one you can see on the cover, had slid a tiny chip into the pocket of her frock without her parents even noticing. It had fallen out into the suitcase. And there it lay, out of sight and out of mind, through all the dreadful things that had begun to happen to her family, one after another, because of the curse.

I had the usual problems that night at home, as well.

'I'm warning you, Melly. This light's going out in five minutes.'

'People your age still need their sleep, you know.'

'Why can't you just put it down, and finish it tomorrow?'

But finally, next morning, I reached the end. Gordon was desperate to have it next, so I made its card out right away, and during library hour I put *Red Rock* on top of the pile of books in front of Imogen.

'Can you stick a yellow dot on this one, so Gordon can take it home today?'

'Sure,' she said, reaching out for it. And then the blood drained from her face. It was extraordinary. I must have read the words a hundred times. *'Her cheeks went pale.' 'Her face went ashen.' 'She turned quite white with shock.'* But I would never in a thousand years have guessed it looked like this. It was as if someone had pulled a plug in the bottom of her feet.

I was sure she was fainting, so I stepped in close, to catch her as she fell. And that's the only reason I was near enough to hear her whispering to the little girl on the book cover.

'No! Not that bit of rock! Don't pick up that one, *please!*'

'Imogen? Imogen!'

It can't have been more than a moment but it seemed an age before she looked up, startled. Her face was still grey and clammy. 'What?'

She hadn't realized that I'd heard what she was whispering.

'Nothing,' I muttered. And it was true that, when it came to saying something, my mind had gone completely blank.

But I was thinking plenty. After all, if it was 'hot off the press', she couldn't possibly have read the book.

So how could she have known what was going to happen?

Chapter Four

That's when I went to talk to Mr Hooper a second time. Don't get me wrong. I love ghost tales as much as anyone. I adore stories in which people have weird dreams, and strange things happen. But that's in books. Real life is supposed to be real, and I like my world to be solid around me. After all, nobody wants to find themselves suddenly trapped in the haunted house they've been watching on television, sensing a presence, and feeling the air going ice-cold around them.

But I was too spooked to go about it the right way. Instead of explaining properly, I just rushed up to Mr Hooper and asked him, 'Can I please dump Imogen now? She knows her way around, and everything.'

He wasn't pleased.

'Melly,' he said to me sternly. 'I've told you before, a week is only a week. Now try and be friendly. It'll be good for you.'

I felt like saying, 'You can talk. You were much nicer to Jason when he was new.' But he'd have thought I was just being cheeky, so I gave up and walked away. And since there was only one more day to go, I tried sticking it out. But it's not easy, sitting next to someone who sees through the covers into books. You can't ask straight out, 'Are you some sort of witch? Do you have second sight?' So I thought I was going about it in a pretty polite and roundabout way when, strolling back from the lunch hall, I said, all casually, 'Imogen, do you believe in looking into the future?'

She spun to face me. 'Looking into the future?'

'You know,' I said. 'Crystal balls and stuff. Knowing about things even before they happen.'

Now she was looking positively hunted. 'Why are you asking?' she demanded. 'Have people been talking about me?'

All the unease I'd been feeling curdled in the pit of my stomach. Either this new girl was a whole lot cleverer at teasing than I'd imagined, or the world was shifting nastily under my feet.

'Tell me you're joking, Imogen.'

You could see that she knew she'd made a big mistake.

'Of course I'm joking,' she tried to backtrack. 'I was just having you on.'

But I could feel hairs rising on the back of my neck, because I knew she was lying.

I looked around. Practically everyone in the class was in the school grounds with us. Why did it have to be *me*?

'Listen, Imogen,' I told her. 'You know that I was only asked to look after you for the first week, not stick like glue for life. And this is our last day, so I'll be taking off now, if that's all right with you.'

I'd have looked hurt, but she looked devastated.

'But, Melly. I thought we were—'

She stopped, and stared down at her feet while the word 'friends' echoed, unspoken, between us. She looked as if she'd been slapped. I couldn't try and pretend that everyone's first-week minder simply strides off halfway through the last day. And I hate lying. So it just popped out.

'I'm sorry, Imogen. I really am. But I can't be friends with you. You're just too *creepy*. I'm too *scared*.'

If someone blurted something like that out in my face, I'd stare in astonishment, and squawk, '*What?*' But Imogen simply looked as if she'd been half expecting it.

'All right,' she said, turning away. 'It doesn't matter.'

'You do understand?'

'Oh, yes,' she said. 'I understand.'

And somehow that made me feel a whole lot worse. Imagine how you'd feel if you refused to be friends with someone who's only ever been perfectly polite and anxious to please, just because they were different or had something wrong with them. And then imagine they said that to you.

Like me, you'd feel an absolute worm.

I stood and watched her walk away. She didn't look back. She didn't even try to pretend she had something to do in the cloakroom. She just set off towards the emptiest part of the school grounds, where she'd be alone. I dug my book out of my bag and turned the other way, to head for the lunchtime library.

And then I thought suddenly: 'Poor Imogen! Now she can't even go there.'

And I felt even *worse*. You see, all the way through school, I've used book corners and lunchtime library to hide away, and spend my break times reading. You know as well as I do that being a bookworm in school is like having a protective shield. It sends a message: 'Please leave me out of things unless I ask. Act as if I'm not here. It's not that I'm lonely. It's just that I'm happy on my own.'

And it is true. I wouldn't want to have to get through even one day the way the others do it. I see them, constantly in each other's company, always cheerful, always chatty. They never get ratty when someone suddenly begins to plait their hair without even asking, or begs to try on their glasses, or pesters them for hours about who is their favourite singer. Twenty different people can come up, one after another, and tell them something they already know, like, 'You've got a cold,' or, 'Those are new shoes you're wearing,' and they keep smiling. They don't even *mind*.

I don't know how they do it. I'd go mad. So making someone feel even a tiny bit awkward about hiding away anywhere, especially the book corner, would be, to me, like snatching away a lifebelt.

I couldn't do it to my own worst enemy. I certainly couldn't do it to someone who'd never done anything except try to be pleasant and helpful.

I had to run after her. 'Imogen! Wait a minute! Stop!'

And she turned and smiled at me. So that was that settled.

Chapter Five

It must have been a good long while since Imogen had had a friend. No-one else wanted to be near her. This was the reason, she admitted, she'd left her old school. Only a few of her classmates had gone around whispering that she was 'creepy' – the ones she thought must have been talking to me – but all of the rest had kept away from her as much as possible, making giant great fusses if they were even asked to share a desk or a table.

'What, even in work groups?'

The tears sprang. 'It was *horrible.*'

I felt so sorry for her. And the teachers had

found her crying in corners so often that, in the end, they had suggested she might be better starting afresh in a new school.

Ours.

The problem was, of course, that you could see it was all happening again, exactly the same. Everyone except me avoided her. It wasn't like giving someone the big freeze because they've been spiteful, or something. In fact, I don't believe people even realized they were doing it. But somehow, everywhere Imogen went, everyone melted away.

And it wasn't just the book corner, because the first time I really noticed it, she and I were walking down the corridor towards the lunch room. Paul had bent down to tie up his shoe-lace, but, as the two of us came close, I saw him hastily straighten up and drift off, with his shoe-lace still flapping.

Funny, I thought.

And then the two girls from another class who had been sitting on the window-ledge, sharing a book, suddenly closed it without a word, and wandered away.

We went into lunch, and, now I'd noticed it, I realized it had been happening all week. Whenever the two of us had headed for a busy table, within seconds everyone was stacking their dishes back onto their trays, and taking them over to the hatches.

Then, on the way back from the cloakroom on my own, I bumped into Maria and Tasj.

'Don't you find it a bit creepy, going round with her?' Tasj asked me outright. 'She's so *weird*.'

'Seriously strange,' agreed Maria.

I tried to defend her. 'She doesn't bother me. I get on with her all right.'

But I was definitely the only one. It wasn't just Mr Hooper who avoided her. Even the other teachers seemed to move away when she was near. That afternoon I stood waiting while Imogen rooted in her book bag to make sure she still had her calculator. Just across the hall, Miss Harvey and Mr Sands were standing together, checking something on a chart. Suddenly, Mr Sands looked quite distracted. He glanced round uneasily, then said to Miss Harvey, 'Shall we go and do this—' He obviously couldn't think of anywhere else they should be doing it, so he just finished up lamely, '—somewhere else?'

I didn't think the idea would go down very well. Miss Harvey's famous in our school for not wasting time. She's usually telling the people in her class what to do even before she walks through the door. But now she, too, was looking round a bit uncomfortably, a bit unsure. And together, still holding the chart, they moved off across the hallway.

Away from their classrooms, I noticed.

Away from Imogen.

And away from me.

So even I ended up having to ask myself how I could stand being so close to someone so spooky. And I can't really explain, except to say that, from the moment I ran after her, she never bothered me at all the way she bothered other people. I never felt the urge to drift away. Now, looking back, I wonder if it was because I was the only one who knew for certain there was something strange about her. I didn't have to share their vague, uneasy feeling. But sometimes I think that all that time spent with my head in books had made weird people so familiar to me that I barely thought twice. After all, no-one writes a story that boils down to, 'Once, there was a normal young girl, and nothing of interest happened her whole life.' And, if they did, no-one would bother to read it. Would you have finished the last book you read if it had been about a plain, happy person doing nothing but plain, happy things?

When you were three, perhaps. Certainly not now.

So I was interested in her. And she turned out to be the perfect friend for someone like me. She was quiet, and she didn't mind spending half her life in the book corner and the other half in the library.

But, though he didn't seem to want to spend too much time near her himself, the fact that she didn't mix with the others did bother Mr Hooper.

'Imogen, maybe you shouldn't be spending all your time skulking between bookshelves like Melly.'

I looked up from the thriller I was reading. 'This is a school,' I teased him. 'You ought to be pleased we're sitting quietly with our noses in books.'

And he never noticed that, though my nose was, hers certainly wasn't. It even took me a while to realize that Imogen never actually read a book. Oh, she'd run her fingertips along the shelves, and pick one out. She had her favourites. One had a country scene on the cover.

"It was so pretty it could have been made of gingerbread..."

Another had children playing happily with puppies and kittens.

"But, best of all, Flora loved Little Fluffy."

She'd settle on one of the little yellow tubs, hold the book in her lap and stare off in the distance. If someone walked past, she'd open what she'd chosen quickly, anywhere, and look down until they'd gone by.

But most of the time she was just sitting with a look of pure enchantment on her face, as if she'd been whisked away somewhere magical.

'Happy?' I'd ask her, and she'd nod dreamily.

Then, 'Happy?' she'd ask me back, and I'd nod as well, because things were going pretty well for me, too, now that Mr Hooper had at last got me down for having a friend, and stopped nagging me about mixing and joining in, and all that stuff.

Yet Imogen kept everyone away.

Especially in swimming. And I love swimming. It's the only sport I like. Mr Hooper says that's because it's practically the only thing we do in school in which I know I'm safe from hearing things like, 'Now get yourselves into two teams,' or 'Choose groups to work in,' or the one that I really loathe, which is, 'Now choose a partner.'

And it is true, I love that feeling when you've finally found a bit of a space in the middle of all that shrieking and splashing. You let your feet slip out in front of you along the tiles, your head slides under, your hair floats up like weed, and just for a moment everyone's vanished. It's just you and your own magical, glistening bubbles.

Then someone steams past, kicking and shrieking, and the world's back again, spoiling it totally.

But Imogen worked like a secret barrier. Nobody except me realized, but from the moment she began picking her way down the steps into the shallows, everyone else was suddenly deciding to practise their racing starts up at the deep end of the pool, or hang by their feet from the bar along the other side.

It was brilliant for me. If I stayed near her, there was so much clear space around us that I could even practise my tumble turns.

'Keep on like this,' said Miss Rorty, 'and you'll win that Harries Cup for sure. I'll put my money on you.'

Over and over I pushed myself back from the side, to try again. And it was only after she blew the whistle, and I was getting out, that I had that really chilling thought.

Miss Rorty was horrified. 'Look at you, child!' she said, snatching up the nearest towel, and wrapping me tight, as if I were one of the infants. 'You're covered in goose-pimples. You're shivering fit to burst!'

But it wasn't cold. I didn't want to explain it, even if I could have done, through chattering teeth. It was something quite different.

The thought had suddenly struck me, getting out, that it was all very well for me to think that there was something weird about Imogen. But what about me?

After all, what would *you* think? How would *you* explain someone not even minding spending half an hour in a corner of the pool which, if they thought about it for a moment, they would have to admit was practically halfway to being haunted?

CHAPTER SIX

Then she came top in something. It was *terri-fying*. We'd just finished reading *Tyke Samuel* together as our book in class. 'Now write an essay,' Mr Hooper said. 'Pretend you're little orphan Sam, sent up to clear the chimneys of some great house. Write what he's thinking.'

I love it when Mr Hooper doesn't spoil things by making us talk about our stories before we write them. I settled down at once, and scribbled frantically till the bell rang. I didn't look up much, but, when I did, I saw that instead of staring round the room as usual, sucking her pencil, Imogen was busily writing, too.

Mr Hooper made Tasj collect them all for him at the end, finished or not, and then we rushed out, because it was going home time. But when we came back in the morning, he was looking thrilled.

'I'm pleased with everyone. Most of you did a good job. But one of the stories was astonishing. Truly outstanding.'

I know it sounds as if I'm being Miss Boastie. But I did really think it must be me.

'Imogen!'

I wasn't the only person to turn and stare. (We all knew how awful her work was.) But no-one could doubt that she'd written every word of it all by herself, because we'd been in the room with her.

Mr Hooper handed her sheets of paper back. 'Go on. Read it out to everyone.'

She fingered her necklace anxiously. 'Oh, no! I couldn't.'

'Of course you can.'

'No, really!'

But Mr Hooper can't stand what he calls 'people being silly'. 'Imogen,' he said in his firm voice. 'Just stop fussing, and read it out to everyone now.'

Her fingers trembled as she held it up in front of her. The pages shook. She started off in such a nervous, stumbling voice that we couldn't make sense of it. She was tripping over some words. She was puzzling over others. You'd think, to watch and listen, she'd never heard a word of it before, let alone written it.

In the end, Mr Hooper had to take pity on her. Stretching towards her, he prised the sheets of paper out of her hands, and went back to his own desk.

There, sitting on the desk, he read it properly.

It made my blood run cold. It was as if Tyke Sam was in the room with us, telling us everything. We sat like mice as he told of his terror of the dark, and how soot fell in showers, blinding him, blocking his ears, and even filling his mouth if he'd been rash enough to open it to gasp, or take a breath between his sobs.

'And once,' he told us, 'I tumbled down the shaft of a chimney into an unswept grate and sent a lady into a fit of screams. I thought I'd startled her out of her wits, because she began to shriek, "Chimney rat! Chimney rat!" over and over.

'But then I realized it was the flying soot that had put her in a fury. And the woman beside her tugged me out from where I crouched, scraped

and bleeding, behind the big brass firescreen, and boxed my poor ears till they rang.'

Everyone shivered. 'They couldn't do that, could they?' Bridie asked. But Mr Hooper didn't answer her. He just read on.

'*I have this fear that grips me. I think I'm going to stick fast so high up that they can't hear my cries. I think they'll wait a day or so. And then decide, for their convenience, it's easier to think that I'm already dead, because it's chilly and they want a fire.'*

That was when Imogen jumped to her feet, and ran from the classroom, holding her hands over her ears.

We all stared at the door she'd left wide open. 'That is so *weird*,' said Bridie. 'If she can *write* something as scary and horrible as that, how come she can't sit and listen when it's read aloud?'

'Perhaps it embarrassed her,' said Mr Hooper. But I knew better. And when he sent me after her, to fetch her back, I told her so.

'That wasn't your story at all, was it? It was still Tyke Sam's.'

She looked up from the cloakroom bench, and snapped defiantly, 'Don't be ridiculous!'

But she'd understood what I meant at once, I noticed. So I persisted. 'It's true, isn't it? You left your hand on the book as you were writing, and he poured his story out through you.'

'That is the silliest—'

'Listen,' I interrupted, pushing Stephen's football gear to the side, and sitting beside her. 'I'm not trying to be rude, but someone like you could no more write a story like that than fly to the moon.'

'I could!'

'No, you couldn't. I know. I sit next to you, remember? *And* I've been watching you.'

The colour crept up, past the gold necklace and up to her cheeks. 'There's nothing to watch!'

'Oh, yes, there is. You're very strange, you know. Everyone senses it. But I think I'm the only one who's begun to fit it together. I think you can see into books. For you, books aren't just imaginary worlds. They're real. Real people, in real places.'

She was still trying to fight back. 'I don't know what you're—'

'Imogen!' I was getting impatient. 'I've guessed your secret. Can't you see? You might as well give up, and tell me all about it. Because you can't just keep on rushing out of classrooms, and changing schools, and finding it so hard to concentrate that all the work you do is rubbish unless some character in a book is writing it for you.'

Her eyes filled up with tears. 'That's *horrible*.'

'It might be horrible, but it's *true*.'

I knew I was winning. 'Listen,' I said to her gently. 'You know you can't carry on like this. You have to talk to somebody. And you can trust me.'

The tears spilled over. She rooted in her pocket to find a tissue, and I sat waiting.

In the end, she turned towards me and looked hard, as if she were working something important out. As if she were *inspecting* me.

And then, suddenly, her face cleared. It was as if the sun had come out inside her. She looked a different person.

'Yes,' she said. 'I think you're right. I think that I can trust you. After all, I'm not the only one who's different. You're different, too, in your own way. What's odd about you is that you're not so tied up with all the others that you have to share secrets. I really do think you could treat it all like just another story in one of your precious books, that you can close when you want. So I can tell you.'

'Right,' I said. 'Story-time. After lunch in the book corner. Deal?'

And Imogen smiled.

'Yes,' she said. 'Deal. After lunch, I'll tell you the story.'

CHAPTER SEVEN

If it were a book, I couldn't put it down, I'll tell you that. I'd find it a real keep-you-upper. Once she had started, out it poured in torrents. How it began when she was tiny, before she could even read. She had been helping her cousin take down the decorations after Christmas, and he was teasing her.

'The youngest person in the house has to wear everything off the tree for a whole week.'

She was so innocent that she believed him. So she stood still while Eddie hooked all of the glittering ornaments off the tree onto her woolly. He draped the tinsel round her, and then, as if she weren't already looking sparkly enough, added a few chocolate Santas and some glitter stars, and then all the rings and bracelets and necklaces he could find in their granny's old jewellery box.

By the time Imogen's mother turned round from the computer, there wasn't an inch of herself, said Imogen, that wasn't twinkling or flashing or jangling.

'Aren't you the Sparkling Lady!' her mother had said admiringly. 'Now come over here, both of you, and take a look at all these Christmas photos.'

Shedding ornaments over the carpet, Imogen rushed to look. Eddie pointed at one of the photographs. 'Look at Aunt Beth, asleep with her mouth open!'

Imogen ran her fingers across the photos on the screen and giggled at Uncle Ted in his paper hat.

Then she said sadly, 'No Aunty Dora.'

Her mother pointed. 'Yes, she's there, sweetheart. Under your finger. And here. And sitting next to the tree in this one.'

But Imogen still looked forlorn, and said again, 'No. No Aunty Dora.'

Now her cousin was getting impatient. 'Don't be silly, Immy.' He stabbed at the screen with his finger. 'She's in this one. And this one.'

Imogen's woolly jangled as she tossed her head. 'Aunty Dora's gone.'

'Gone where, sweetheart?'

But there was no way Imogen could explain. And her mother had stopped trying to listen even before the phone rang with the terrible news.

'That's awful,' I said. 'So did your mother guess?'

'Not then,' said Imogen. 'It was only when it happened a second time, ages later, that she thought back and remembered that morning with the Christmas photos.'

'Why? Was the second time the same sort of thing?'

'No. It was different. But it was just as *strange*. I'd had a horrible day. I'd lost the toss in my ballet class, and couldn't be the princess in the show.' She grinned, embarrassed. 'I came home in *floods*. Mum did her best. "You be a princess for *me*," she said. So I dressed up and started dancing. But it was stupid, so I ended up in tears again. Mum pulled me onto her lap, and read me a story about a little pit pony called Patch. And suddenly I was going mad, struggling and screaming about water closing over Patch's head. And when we got further into the story—'

'I know,' I told her. 'I had that book, too. That's a horrible bit, when he falls in the water.'

"And it seemed to poor Patch that he would never again reach firm ground..."

Imogen shivered. 'Well, next day, when I was calm again, and we reached that part in the story, Mum stopped and gave me a funny look. "You knew this, didn't you?" And that's when she guessed.'

'My mum would just have thought I'd had the book read to me in school.'

'I think mine would have thought that, except that she says she's always had a bit of a gift that way herself.'

'I'm not sure why she'd call it a "gift",' I said.

Imogen looked blank.

I tried to explain. 'I don't mean to be rude, but most of the time your work is *terrible*, and half of the books in the school give you the frights. On top of that, it seems that if you don't watch out where you're putting your fingers, you know in advance when terrible things are going to happen – in books *and* in real life.' I spread my hands. 'Hardly a gift,' I continued. 'More like some sort of *blight*.'

From the look on her face you'd have thought that I'd said she had some mangy disease, or something. She looked so upset I had to change the subject quickly.

'So how does it work, then, this strange gift of yours?'

'Work?' The question puzzled her a little. 'Well, it's a sort of imagining. Like in a dream.'

'What sort of dream?'

'Depends. If the book that I'm touching is happy, then it's lovely. Like being there, but on a cloud. In things, but not quite.'

'Like reading,' I said. 'Like being lost in a book.'

'*More*,' she insisted. And I remembered all the times I'd seen her sitting lost in a rapturous world of her own.

'How?' I asked. 'I mean, suppose you were holding *Tansy at St Clare's?*'

'You might dream the midnight feast bit. You'd smell the cakes, and feel a part of the chatter around you.

"'We'll do it eeny meeny miny mo,' said Laura..."

'Or if it was *Philippa and the Midnight Pony*, you'd feel the cold air on your face, the hooves thudding beneath you, and all the excitement.'

Then I remembered all the times she'd acted as if she'd practically been bitten.

'So what if it's a chiller thriller, or a horror book?'

'Oh, then it's *awful*, like being trapped in a nightmare. You have all these horrible and panicky feelings as you see every ghastly thing about to happen, like a train coming round the bend while the car's still stuck on the crossing, or the toddler leaning too far out of the top-floor window. But, just like in a bad dream, there's nothing you can do to help. You just have to stand there, holding your breath, and watching and waiting.'

'You can't *ever* stop it?'

'No. Because it's already there, in the words on the page.'

I thought for a bit. Then I said, 'You take that book, *Clown Colin*—'

She waved her hands frantically in front of her face. 'No! Don't! I hate even thinking about when his wooden eyes start spinning round and round. Don't even talk about it!'

I tried another one. 'How about *Little Mattie*?'

'Noo-oo!' she wailed. 'That bit where he's dragged away from his mum – I can't *bear* it!'

"...until he couldn't even see her any more."

That is so *weird*, I thought. And I couldn't have felt more sorry for her. After all, I read more than my fair share of books that make me keep the light on all night long. And lots of books that make me sad, or anxious, till things work out right. But I don't end up in a state like her, half-way to fainting because of three or four grisly pages, and not even able to look at the cover of that book ever again without wanting to shudder.

'A gift', her mother called it. But, the more Imogen told me about it, the more I thought that that was totally the wrong word.

'Curse' was more like it.

Yes. Not 'gift', but 'curse'.

CHAPTER EIGHT

I had a hundred more questions, but the bell had rung, and when we got back to the classroom, Mr Hooper was in one of his 'Time-to-start-something-new' moods.

'*Compare and Contrast*,' he announced. And through the long afternoon we tried it with fifty different things: light and dark, noise and silence, misery and happiness, on and on and on.

'And that's your homework,' he told us afterwards. 'One and a half pages of Compare and Contrast.'

'Can we do anything?' I asked him.

'Anything.'

'And can it be private?'

'I suppose so.'

(For 'Private', you put a large red P up in the top corner. Then, even if it's the best piece of work in the class, he won't read it out to everyone.)

I had a plan. As we left class, I said to Imogen, 'Shall I walk home with you? I'll come as far as your house, and then cut back through Stannard's car park.'

She seemed so pleased, I felt a little guilty. And I felt worse when Mr Hooper, who'd been listening, whispered in my ear, 'See? Wasn't I right? Once you get used to it, it's nice to have company.'

But even knowing I was using her to do my homework didn't stop me asking her questions all the way back to her house.

'Was your mum pleased when she realized you could see into books and photos? Or was she horrified?'

'She was excited,' Imogen admitted. 'I think people always teased her when she said she knew things were going to happen. So I think she was pleased I took after her a little bit.'

'Does she encourage it?'

'Encourage it?'

I tried to explain. 'When my mum realized I was good at swimming, she signed me up at swim club right away. But when she found out I could crack my fingers, she couldn't stop me fast enough. "Don't do that!" she kept saying. "It's a horrible habit!"'

Imogen considered. 'But this isn't like either of those things. It just happens, or it doesn't.'

'Is that what your mum thinks?'

'I suppose so.'

'So she doesn't go round shoving books at you, just out of curiosity, to see what happens?'

'Of course she doesn't.'

'But she hasn't done anything to put a stop to it, either?'

Imogen stared. 'Like *what*?'

I couldn't think of anything, anyhow. Somehow, when it came down to it, it hardly seemed polite to mention going to doctors, or hypnotists, or psychiatrists, or anything like that. And anyhow, maybe Imogen and her mother were right, and being able to see into books and photos was one of those things, like blue eyes or freckles, that you couldn't do anything about if you wanted.

So I just kept on with the questions, ticking the answers off in my head, ready for later.

'Well, does it worry her that it's so hard for you to concentrate on your schoolwork?'

'I try not to say too much about that,' Imogen admitted.

'But she must know you're having problems.

What about when you had to change schools because people thought you were—' I would have said 'creepy', but it seemed nicer to finish up '– a little *strange*?'

'She was surprised it all got so difficult so quickly.'

'Did it?'

'Oh, yes. Before last year, it only ever happened those two times – with Aunty Dora's photo, and that book about the pony. I still had plenty of friends. And my work wasn't bad, either.'

That made sense. After all, she'd written out that story from Tyke Sam pretty fast, covering three whole pages in less than half an hour. And Mr Hooper could read it.

'So this whole business just got worse suddenly?'

'Yes,' Imogen said. 'And maybe one day it'll go away again just as quickly.'

'Would you like that?'

She didn't answer. She just stared ahead.

'How about your mum?' I asked. 'Would *she* like it?'

'Why are you asking all these questions?' Imogen burst out.

I shut up, fast, in case she guessed. But anyway, we were already turning the corner into her road. Imogen led me past three or four plain, boring old houses, then up the path beside another, just the same.

'Mum's probably round the back,' she said, pushing open the side gate. I followed her through, and stopped in my tracks, astonished. The back of the house was amazing. I just *stared*.

How to describe it? It looked as if fairies and goblins had decorated the whole place for a joke. The bricks were yellow, the door red, the window frames green and their shutters blue. All over the lawn were tiny pretend windmills, and gnomes fishing in ponds, and plaster tortoises and rabbits. There was even a wizard sitting cross-legged on a stone mushroom, waving his wand. If you were five, you would have thought you'd fallen through a hole in the real world, and ended up in a Toytown picture book.

'That is incredible!'

Behind me, there was an excited voice. 'Do you really like it? *Really?*'

I spun round.

'Melly,' said Imogen. 'This is my mum.'

She didn't look like anybody's mum to me. She was so *young*, and tall and bright-eyed, with blazing red hair tumbling over her shoulders like lava spilling out of a volcano. She wore a bright shawl, embroidered with sparkling butterflies, and when she reached out to fold her arms tightly round Imogen, to hug her, Imogen practically vanished beneath the butterflies and the waterfall of hair.

'Good day, my precious?'

I don't know what I was expecting Imogen to say. Maybe if I had someone from school standing there listening, I wouldn't start by launching into a great long wail about what Tyke Sam made me write being so horrid I had to leave the classroom.

But still I wouldn't have answered, like she did, 'It was lovely, Mum. Really good.' And sounded as if she meant it. I didn't know if it was because of me that she said nothing, or if she was putting a brave face on her horrible day to hide from her mother the fact that she'd cracked, and told her secret to someone outside the family.

But, whichever it was, her mother believed her. Her bright eyes twinkled happily. She tossed her hair back, and, releasing poor Imogen from her grasp, held her at arm's length like a toddler, peered in her eyes, and asked hopefully,

'And did anything "special" happen?'

I stared. My mum asks, 'Anything special happen?' But she's not really paying attention. If I answered, 'Yes, Mr Hooper fell off the roof and broke his neck,' she'd stop clattering pans around long enough to listen. And if I said, 'Yes, everyone teased me till I cried,' she'd be on the phone to Mrs Trent in a flash. But mostly, she asks casually. She's only checking. If something really interesting or funny happened, she wants to hear about it. But that's all.

But this was different. Imogen's mother's 'Anything "special" happen?' was clearly code for their little shared secret. I waited for Imogen to tell her. But she just shook her head.

And Mrs Tate looked really disappointed.

'Well, never mind,' she said, in that exact same tone Miss Rorty uses when I don't make my best time in the pool. 'Never mind.' She turned to me, and her face brightened. 'A visitor! How lovely!' She clapped her hands like someone in a pantomime. 'We must have iced cakes and home-made lemonade!'

'I really ought to be pushing off home now,' I told her. 'My mum will be—'

But she'd danced off. I mean it. She was literally dancing up the garden path, flapping her shawl like a giant great butterfly. I glanced across at Imogen, but she clearly hadn't even noticed I thought her mother was a little odd. And I can understand that. After all, if she came round to our house unexpectedly, and caught my mum all ratty and irritable because she's worried about money, or about Granny going back into hospital, she'd probably think our house was strange, and I wouldn't notice.

But there was certainly nothing ratty about Mrs Tate. Having tea with her and Imogen was like stepping into one of those old books you sometimes find in charity shops, with thick spongy paper and coloured illustrations hidden under tissue. Everything was 'thrilling', or 'perfectly wonderful', or 'absolutely scrumptious', or 'such, such fun!'

I couldn't wait to get away, back to my own mum.

She wasn't too pleased with me. 'Next time you're going to be an hour late, don't just leave a message to *tell* me. Ask me the day *before*.'

'I'm sorry,' I said, and rushed into some story about Imogen really needing someone to walk her home. But it was still a good half-hour before she'd calmed down enough for me to get on with this homework I was planning.

'What would you do if you found I could see into books?'

'See into books?'

'And photos.'

Mum's used to weird questions from me, depending on what I'm reading. But you could tell that this one baffled her.

'What do you mean?'

'Well,' I explained. 'Suppose each time I touched a book, I knew exactly what was in it.'

She gave a little snort of amusement. 'Now wouldn't your teachers all be pleased with that!'

'But it felt real. And sometimes it upset me.'

'Like when you read that ghastly book about that badger?'

'Much worse than that.'

Mum gave me a look. We both remembered what I was like, reading that badger book. She kept on trying to tug it away, but I kept snatching it back because, once I'd got started, I had to know what happened. But I couldn't stop crying, right through to the horrible end. And the minute I'd finished, Mum stuffed it in the dustbin.

"And every leaf that rustled seemed to shriek 'Danger!'"

'Well,' she said thoughtfully. 'If it was going to be worse than that, I couldn't be doing with it.'

'What about the photos? Suppose I could tell how everyone in a photo was going to end up?'

'You mean, look at a school photograph, and be able to tell who'd end up in jail, and who'd end up prime minister?'

'That sort of thing.'

She shuddered. 'I can't imagine anything worse than being able to see into the future.'

'You wouldn't call it a gift, then?'

'No, I certainly wouldn't. It sounds terrible.'

'And you wouldn't encourage it?'

'*Encourage* it? I think I'd forbid it!'

'You can't forbid magic,' I reminded her.

'Oh, *can't* you?' said my mum, in such a determined '*I* could' tone of voice that I was practically assured on the spot that, if I'd been unlucky enough to be born with a gift like Imogen's, my mother would have splatted it flat in my cradle.

And wasn't I glad about that!

CHAPTER NINE

I was called up to the desk about my homework. Mr Hooper swung round in his chair till we both had our backs to everyone.

'Is this your idea of being a *friend*?' he asked me crossly, flapping my 'Compare and Contrast' work under my nose.

'I told you it was private,' I said stubbornly. 'And I put on a giant *P*.'

'Melly, this piece is *horrible*.'

'It's *true*,' I argued.

'But you can't write things just because they're *true*.'

'That's the whole *point* of writing,' I explained.

'Books say they're made up, but they're actually a lot more truthful than real life.'

'What do you mean?'

'Well, look,' I said. 'People feel *safer* if it's in a book. You can read about the most terrible people, and hardly think twice about it. But if you hear something even a quarter as bad about someone you know in real life, everyone goes bananas.' I pointed at my homework. 'See?'

That shut him up.

'*And,*' I went on, 'you know what's going on better in books.' I pointed over at Imogen. 'I'd have a whole lot better idea of what was going on in her house, and inside her head, if she were in a book. At least the person who wrote it wouldn't be too polite to tell me. As it is, I just have to *guess.*'

'Melly,' he told me sternly, 'I didn't try and help you make a friend just so you could start being nosy about her private life.'

'I thought people were supposed to be interested in their friends.'

'Interested, yes. Nosy, certainly not.'

'I don't see any difference.'

He couldn't explain it, that was obvious. He flicked the pages I'd written between his fingers once or twice, staring at me anxiously, while I thought how *useful* it would be to have an author around all the time to explain people properly, without all that stuff that everyone knows is not true really but feels they ought to say to be polite, like, 'Oh, I'm sure she didn't *mean* it', or, 'I expect she just forgot, dear', or, 'No, she likes you *really*'. Authors are braver, and more honest. They would explain why Imogen's mother was too wrapped up in planting silly joke gardens and thinking everything was fun and jolly, even to notice her daughter was being driven crazy because she'd had such a horrible gift passed on to her.

A gift passed on . . .

'Mel?' Mr Hooper was still staring at me.

'Sorry,' I said hastily. But still the words snagged in my brain. 'A gift passed on . . .' They were reminding me of something, but I couldn't think what.

Now Mr Hooper was sighing. 'You just don't get it, do you, Mel?'

'No.' I was getting irritable myself now. 'And I

don't think it's fair, you ticking me off like this. You said, "Compare and Contrast". You said we could do anything. And you agreed it could be private. I haven't shown my work to Imogen. I haven't hurt her feelings. I just chose something interesting, thought about it hard, and wrote it properly.'

'But, really, Mel! To write a piece about how your two mums are so different!' He peered at the top page in his hand. *"My mum might be horribly ratty, but at least she has a grip. You can depend on her."* And fancy writing—' Again, he searched the page for the bit that had upset him. *"It must be awful having Mrs Tate as a mother. She might be the sort of person who can make a rainy picnic fun, or giggle about anything. But you couldn't come to her with a problem. She'd just pretend it wasn't there, or didn't matter."'*

'She would, too,' I insisted. 'Maybe you haven't met her, but I have.'

He slid the paper-clip off my pages, and folded them over and over till they were small enough to fit in his trouser pocket.

'This isn't going in your folder,' he said. 'I'm burning it. I'm not going to run the risk of Imogen ever seeing it.'

'Fine by me.'

'And you're to promise me you'll never mention it.'

'I promise.'

'Cross your heart?'

'Cross my heart.'

He gave me a good long look, and you could tell that what he really wanted to say was, 'Mel, you're so *weird*.' But he controlled himself.

'Right,' he said, swivelling back to face the rest of the class. 'This discussion is over.'

'Except—' I reminded him.

'Except?'

'My mark,' I said. 'You haven't told me what I got for it.'

Back came the stern look. 'Melly,' he said, 'I wouldn't mark this if you paid me my weight in gold.'

'But, if you *did* . . .?' I persisted.

He rolled his eyes. 'Mel, you're *incorrigible*.'

'Just tell me,' I begged. 'After all, I spent a good long time on it, and did it as well as I could.'

'Oh, very well!' he snapped. 'Since you have promised you'll never mention it again, I'll tell you what you would have got for it.'

I waited, knowing. And I was dead right.

Ten out of ten. Perfect *A*. Excellent!

Goody.

Chapter Ten

That afternoon, Imogen ended up in tears again. Our class was picking teams for indoor games. Arinda and Luke were calling.

'Tom.'

'Matty.'

'Pats. No! Sorry, I've changed my mind. Louay!'

'Then I'll have Pats.'

As I expected, Imogen was left even till after me. But, at the end, when he was still one person down, Luke turned away and started making plans. 'Who wants to be shooter?'

Me? I'd have been delighted if it happened. By the time Mrs Tallentire came back with the team sashes and ball, I'd have been tucked in the gap under the gym stairs, quietly reading. And if she was cross with me, I'd have been ready to argue. 'Well, what was I *supposed* to do? Nobody picked me.'

But Imogen stood there, drooping. ('Like a lily in a flood', as Mr Hooper calls it.) Her eyes were bright with tears. No-one in our class is positively spiteful. It was the old 'drift-away' business working again. Nobody else even noticed, not even Mrs Tallentire, who hardly gave Imogen a glance, let alone one of the sashes. So she did end up on our team, but on the very edge, along the wall, and I don't think the ball was thrown in her direction once, for the whole game.

'That's it!' I told her, after. 'Tomorrow, after school, we're off to the library.'

'The town library? Why?'

'You'll see.'

She kept up the pestering, but I wouldn't tell, in case she wouldn't come. Next day, we walked straight up the stairs to *Reference*, and still she hadn't guessed why we were there. I left her staring at the huge Map of World Animals while I got started.

Magic. Superstitions. Legends. If you don't believe them, then they're fascinating. I've sat for hours hunched over tales of banshees wailing to warn of deaths on the way, and soldiers who had died at midnight in a field hospital along the line scaring the wits out of their fellow officers by turning up again on the dawn watch.

But if, like me, you have begun to think you're practically living in one of these stories, you're looking for something different. And it wasn't there. I ran my eyes down list after list on the computer screen, and scoured shelf after shelf. There were whole books on tarot cards and palm-reading, half a bookcase on haunted houses, tomes on black magic and spell-making, lots about poltergeists, even a pamphlet on spirit-writing.

But nothing at all about giving it up.

Imogen wasn't helping. 'Look, Melly,' she kept saying. 'This isn't your problem. Stop worrying about me. I'm perfectly happy with things the way they are.'

'Oh, yes?'

'Yes.' She made a face. 'I know it's all sometimes a little bit upsetting—'

'A little bit *upsetting*?' I stared down from where I was balancing on one of the stumpy little library ladders. 'You practically *fall* into the most upsetting books. You even know when members of your family are coasting towards accidents. Everyone avoids you, and you can't even get on with your work. And you call that "a little bit upsetting"? Well, you must have nerves of steel.'

'All right!' she flared. 'Sometimes it's horrible, and I can't sleep at nights. But I still can't see what you're hoping to find in all these books.'

I reached up higher, to pull a couple of books without titles on their spines off the top shelf. 'Listen, Imogen. There has to be some way you can get out of this.'

'Get out of it?'

'Lose this "gift" of yours. Turn back into a normal person.'

'I *am* a normal person!'

'You know what I mean. And if your mum's right, and what you've got is like blue eyes, or curly hair, then you can't be the first.'

'So what are you looking for?'

'A book,' I said. 'I'll know it when I find it. It'll be something that explains what all the people who were like you before did to get rid of it.'

She looked quite blank.

'Listen,' I told her patiently. 'You don't think you're the first of your sort to be unpopular, do you? I'm sure seeing into the future has never been the best way of making and keeping friends. Don't tell me all those early soothsayers were daft enough to stroll around turning ashen every five minutes, and pointing at the next person who was going to fall down the well, because I don't believe it. The rest of the villagers would have stood for it only once or twice, and then drowned them in the duckpond.'

Imogen was silent. I do believe it must have been the very first time she'd given a thought to all the people who'd had the gift in centuries before. But that's one of the things you get from reading all the time – a sense of other places, other times, and other ways of doing things.

'So what are you telling me?' she asked at last.

'I'm not telling you anything,' I said, 'because I don't yet know. But you can be pretty sure that, whatever it is you want to find out about, somebody wanted to know it before you. And books have been invented for over four hundred years. So there's usually one about it somewhere.'

Again, I reached up to the very top shelf, this time for a volume called *Magical Thinking* which had caught my attention.

'My bet', I told her, 'is that most of these special people must have had the sense to lose this so-called "gift" of theirs as fast as they could. And I'm going to find out how they did it.'

'I bet they didn't *all* want to lose it,' she said stubbornly. 'I bet some of them thought that it was *interesting*.'

'Or *fun*,' I said scathingly. 'People like your mother.'

I heard the sharp intake of breath. But, struggling with my balance on the top step, I must have missed the sound of her footsteps walking away, and the swish of the swing doors closing behind her.

That, or another of her skills was Levitation. Or even Vanishing. Because, when I looked round again, Imogen had gone.

CHAPTER ELEVEN

When someone storms off like that, you're not quite sure if they've gone off for good, or if they're going to show up again in a few minutes, pretending they just went off to buy sweeties or gum.

So I sat on the ladder a little while, hoping she'd reappear, and flicking through *Magical Thinking* by Prof. J. B. Blackstaffe. It was a bit of a surprise, that book. You'd think someone like me, who reads so much, would have got used to the fact that titles so often turn out to mean something quite different from what you imagined when you first saw them on the shelf. I would have thought that *Magical Thinking* would be about spells, or the power of thought, or voodoo, or something.

In fact, it was poor old Professor Blackstaffe trying to persuade us to use our brains.

He posed little problems at the top of each page, and asked you questions. Then he told you what the Great Thinkers of the Past would have thought about each one.

While I was waiting for Imogen, I read the first.

> *Your good friend is wasting time in terrible company. One day, the wastrels move, and ask you to pass on their new address and phone number.*
>
> *Do you:*
> *A: Refuse to accept the task?*
> *B: Take the details, rip them up, and say nothing?*
> *C: Pass the information on, with your usual warning?*

Most of the Great Thinkers of the Past turned out to be Stellar Fusspots, too, if you want my opinion. They mostly went for *A* or *C*. (I'd have picked *B*.) But when it was obvious Imogen wasn't coming, I gave up and put the book back on the shelf, and went on home.

I hoped by morning she'd have forgiven me for being so rude about her mother. But when I took my place beside her in the class, she turned away.

I tapped her shoulder. 'Look,' I said. 'That was a horrible thing I said, and I'm really sorry. But I was only trying to help you.'

'*Help* me?' She glowered. 'You mean, *bully* me, don't you?'

I stared at her. 'Is that really what you think I've been doing?'

'Well, isn't it? Dragging me off to the library when you can't find exactly what you want here in school? Making me hang around while you peer into every single book?'

'I'm only trying to find something that has to be there.'

Her eyes flashed. 'Oh, yes! It has to be there, of course! You know! And that's the trouble with you, Melanie Palmer. You think you know *everything*. But it doesn't even seem to have sunk into your big, fat, book-swollen brain that in that library there were about a billion books about harnessing the ancient mysteries, but none at all about giving it up!'

And she was rumbled. I had rumbled her. It's *words*, you see. Miss Rorty knows the spin on a ball. Mum senses when I'm coming down with something. Mr Hooper knows when someone's had too much help with their homework.

And I know words. I know exactly how they fit, and where they belong. I know who uses which ones, and I can always sense when they are out of place.

Or have been borrowed.

'"*Harnessing the ancient mysteries*"? Is that what your mother calls it?'

It was as if I'd pressed some button that said, '*Detonate!*' She went berserk. Tears spurted, and she flew at me, practically pushing me backwards off my chair.

'Shut up! My family's nothing to do with you! So just shut up!'

And don't we all know those words, too! Neil used to yell them all the time when his dad went to prison, and people in the classroom made even friendly remarks, or asked even reasonable questions. So now I at least had a clue to why Imogen kept secrets from her giddy, childlike mother, and hid the strains of all her days in school, and tried to keep pleasing with this horrible 'gift' of hers.

Like Neil, she was just trying to protect someone she loved who couldn't help but embarrass her.

And she had made enough noise doing it. Now everyone was staring. And when Mr Hooper came in through the door a moment later, his eyebrows were already raised. He must have heard from outside in the corridor.

I didn't want to make things worse for her. So I just tried to make a joke of it, moving my chair back and raising my arms, like someone protecting themselves from an attacker. But to her, I whispered, 'Sorry! I'm really sorry. I didn't mean to say anything nasty. I just thought it didn't sound like you. But I wasn't being rude about your mother again, honestly. In fact—'

If you'd seen her tearful face, you'd have lied too.

'In fact, I'm sure she's right. She knows an awful lot more than I do, after all, having a bit of a gift herself. I only dragged you to the library because I was *curious.*'

Mollified, Imogen stopped scowling so fiercely.

'Friends?' I asked tentatively.

There was a moment's silence, then, 'All right, then. Friends,' she agreed, a little unwillingly.

I didn't like to push it, so I was good as gold all day. Mr Hooper helped. Twice, he sent me off on good long jobs, to give us a rest from each other. But things were still a little prickly, so when she rather diffidently asked me if I wanted to walk home with her, I didn't like to tell her it was my swimming evening and I didn't have time, so I invited her along instead.

'We practically drive down your street. Mum won't mind stopping to pick you up.'

In fact, Mum was delighted. (Like Mr Hooper, she's always relieved to find I'm not completely allergic to spending time with real people.) So, even though you could tell that something about Imogen made her a bit uneasy, she was nice to her all the way, asking her how she was enjoying being in a new school, and whether she was getting along with Mr Hooper, and what she liked doing best – even trying to get Imogen into the pool as an extra on our Family Swimsaver Ticket.

While the man at the cash desk was reaching down our locker key bracelets, Imogen and I stood back against the wall. I pointed to one of the framed photographs opposite.

'That looks exactly like the Harries Cup.'

Imogen grinned. 'You really want to win it, don't you, Mel?'

'I've wanted it for *three years*,' I confessed. 'The first year, Toby Harrison beat me by a couple of metres. That was fair enough. Then, last year, Mum wouldn't even let me try.'

Imogen stared across at my mum. 'Wouldn't *let* you?'

'I did have flu,' I admitted. 'But still I'm sure I could have done it. There was only Phoebe Tucker in the running, and I was a good five seconds faster than her over the whole three lengths. But this year she's too old to enter. So,' I said, flattening myself back against the wall to let a man with a pushchair get past, 'in two weeks' time, Mr

Archibald Leroy, Councillor for Leisure Services, will be handing the Harries Cup to *me*.'

'No, he won't,' said Imogen.

'Sorry?'

I'd turned to stare at her, but just at that moment, Mum hurried over. 'What a time that took! Let's hope there's no more messing about, or it won't have been worth coming.' She held out her cupped hands. 'Right, then. Hand it all over. Money, watches, diamonds . . .'

She makes the same joke every week. I slid off my watch, and passed it across.

'And you, dear.' Mum turned to Imogen. 'What about that necklace?'

Imogen patted it. 'No, really. It's all right. I always swim in it. The clasp's so stiff it never comes undone by accident.'

'I'm not sure that's wise,' Mum said. 'It's one thing wearing it in a school lesson, when everyone knows it's yours. But this session is different.'

'All right.' Imogen turned her back to me. 'Can you get it undone, Mel?'

I struggled with the clasp. She was quite right, it was horribly stiff and difficult. But finally I managed to prise it open. The slim gold chain fell like a tiny living snake into my palm. It was so cold, it startled me. And though I was sure it was imagination, it seemed to stir of its own accord, even before I prodded it with my finger.

'What are those strange scratches on it?' Mum asked, opening her bag for me to spill the glittering loops of gold safely inside.

'My mother says they're charms,' said Imogen. 'The wavy shapes stand for water, and the pointy ones for roots.'

'Curious,' said Mum, snapping her bag shut. 'And much safer here with me than in those lockers.' She set off up the stairs for the café, and I turned to Imogen.

'Why did you *say* that?' I demanded.

'About the roots and water?'

'No,' I said. 'About Councillor Leroy not being there to give me the Harries Cup.'

'I didn't say that. All I said was—'

She stopped, and stared at me, appalled. I couldn't work out what was wrong with her. It wasn't quite like all the times before, when blood drained from her face. But she still looked horrified enough.

'Oh, no!' she whispered, her eyes on me, huge and round.

'What's up?' I asked her. 'Is it bad news about Councillor Leroy? Is he going to *die?*'

She shook her head and tried to pull herself together. But though she tried to answer sensibly, she still looked weird. Not scared, exactly. More sort of cagey. Shifty-looking, even.

'What's going on?' I demanded. 'Imogen, what's going on?'

She took a breath and said firmly: 'Nothing. Nothing at all.' But she was still looking hunted, and, desperate to distract me, she glanced around.

'Oh, look!' She pointed to the label under the photograph on the wall behind. 'That's who we're talking about – Councillor Leroy.'

And that's when I guessed what had happened. While we were leaning back against the wall to let the father with the pushchair pass, her head must have brushed against the photo. But if, from that, she knew he wouldn't be the one to give me the Harries Cup, she must have known what was going to happen to him. And I like Mr Leroy. He was so kind the year that Toby beat me, managing to make me smile even though I was close to crying. And Mrs Trent says he even remembered to ask after me when I wasn't there last year. I wouldn't like to think of him as ill. Or *worse.*

'So why won't he be there?'

Imogen said uneasily, 'Mel, I don't know. *Honestly.*'

I don't think I've ever heard anyone say the word 'honestly' more as if they were lying. But this was no time to start a quarrel. If I had raised my voice, it would have echoed up over the balcony, and Mum would have hurried down from the café to chew me out for being so rude to someone I'd invited.

Scowling, I turned away. And then I thought: Well, fair's fair. She might be hiding something, but there are things I don't tell her. She didn't know I liked her near me in the pool because the fact that she kept everyone away gave me more room to practise.

Cheered, I lifted my bag of swimming things. 'Come on,' I said, grabbing her arm. 'All this is wasting good swimming time. Let's hurry up and get changed, and get in the water so I can get on with my tumble turns.'

And, filled with relief at being let off the hook, she rushed after me through the swing doors.

CHAPTER TWELVE

Not that the great clear-a-space-around-us plan was working properly. It was so irritating. From the moment we stepped in the changing rooms, we were surrounded. First, Imogen got caught up in a game with the small children in the next cubicle.

'Knicker-snatcher! Knicker-snatcher!'

I heard them giggling the whole time I was getting into my swimsuit. And even as Imogen and I went through the tunnel to the footbaths, their squeals were echoing off the tiles.

But I was sure that, once we were in the water, everyone would drift away as usual. How wrong I was. Imogen splashed into the shallow end, gasping as she got used to the water, and suddenly she was being mobbed by excited children, all shrieking and calling to her, and it was obvious that if I was going to find room to practise, I'd do far better up the other end.

'See you in a bit.'

I looked up after every tumble turn, thinking her usual magic would have worked, and there'd be space around her. But it got worse. Each minute that passed, more children gathered, desperate to join in the game she was inventing. 'Can *I* play? Can *I* play?' And, by the time I'd finished practising, she even had a group of parents floating lazily on their backs a few feet away from her, taking advantage of the fact that here in the pool today was the most brilliant unpaid nanny.

'Mel! Melly! Over here!'

She'd seen I'd finished. Still, I took my time, watching her curiously as I stroked my way through the water towards her. She looked like a different Imogen suddenly, standing taller, and swinging the children round, bursting with energy.

'Mel! Come and help! I *need* you.'

At her imperious command, I swam a little faster. But once I reached the circle, instead of joining it I arched up and plunged under to play the shark around the little forest of waving legs. Standing knee-deep in churning water shrieking with laughter is certainly not my idea of fun.

But no-one can stay for ever under water. So, in the end, I had to surface to face this merry, bright-eyed person who'd been turning things into a glorious play-time.

Just like her mother . . .

And that, of course, is when I realized. Splashing to her side, I pulled her round to face me. 'It's that *necklace*, isn't it?'

'Sorry?'

Peeling strands of wet hair from across her eyes, she stared.

'That necklace you're not wearing at the moment! That's what's making you—'

'Making me what?'

'You know.' There was no other way of putting it. 'Creepy. You've taken it off, and now you're a different person. No-one would recognize you. Look at you! You're—'

But little hands were grabbing at her. She swung around to face a dozen shining wet faces, all yelling.

'Imogen, come back!'

'Swing me again!'

'Don't go off now!'

Imogen turned back to me, distracted and torn. 'That can't be right,' she said. 'Don't forget everything started *years* before I was given the necklace.'

'Yes, maybe it did,' I said. 'But—'

Then something made me stop – right there. Go carefully, I warned myself. If Imogen's mother can't see that she once had a totally different sort of daughter – ablaze with life – then she must really have her mind set on this magic stuff. Melly, you might have to sort all this out yourself. Don't forget Professor Blackstaffe says in his book that 'knowledge is power'. So maybe it's best not to give too much away.

'Oh, *right*!' I said. 'Stupid of me. I'd forgotten

you'd already had those visions earlier, when you were younger.'

She didn't notice anything suspicious. And anyway, the children were still clamouring. 'Imogen! Swing me!'

She picked up the nearest child and swung her round. Quickly, I copied her. 'Who wants the next go? Queue up! Queue up!'

As I said, standing in circles shrieking with merriment is not my idea of a good time. But I did stick it for a good half hour, rather than have Imogen even remember what it was that I'd just said before her little friends distracted her.

Or begin to suspect what it was I was thinking.

CHAPTER THIRTEEN

Of course she thought that wearing the necklace had nothing to do with it. Imogen wasn't a reader. If you don't read, you don't get all that practice in picking up clues, and making up pictures in your head of how things must have happened. I'd suddenly imagined her exactly as she'd described herself when she was little, standing by the Christmas tree, sparkling all over because her cousin was hooking every glittery thing that he could find onto her somewhere.

Every glittery thing . . .

Then, just a couple of years later, in the very

same room, dancing a private princess dance for her mother. She'd have her tutu on, of course. And her pink ballet slippers. But to dress up to look the part, surely the first place she'd have gone was the old jewellery box. With the help of some hairgrips, even the slinkiest of gold chains can be made to look like a tiara.

And then, last year, on her birthday, what was she given? (Because around then is when she said all this started in earnest.) The very day she took the desk beside me, she'd said, 'My granny gave it to my mother, and now she's passed it on to me.'

I know my mother wouldn't pass on something like that, unless the day was very special.

What day's more special than your birthday?

'*First, check your working,*' Mr Hooper says. So, in the changing rooms, I asked her casually,

'What should I ask for on my birthday?'

'Melly, your birthday's not for *months.*'

'I know,' I said. 'But I like thinking about it. What did you get last year?'

Her eyes shone with the memory. 'A trip to London. We saw *Copacabana!*'

'Brilliant! What did you wear?'

'Well, we were in posh seats. So I wore my blue top and red velvet skirt.'

'What about jewellery?'

She thought back. 'Earrings. And my necklace,

of course, because I'd just been given that. Oh, yes. And my swirly snake ring.'

'*If there's time, check twice,*' says Mr Hooper. So on the way out of my cubicle, I pulled my new library book out of my bag and rested it on top, ready. Then I made sure that when Mum undid her handbag, I was at her side.

'Here you are, Mel,' she said, holding my watch out. But I ignored it totally, and slipped my hand inside her bag, to fish out the necklace.

Again, it was cold, and almost too slinky to the touch. I didn't drop it, though. I kept a grip as I held it out towards Imogen and pretended to stumble. And, as I fell, I laid my hand flat on the library book.

Wolf!

Such a howling! I could barely hear for baying in my ears. And sounds of yelping and snapping. It was *horrible*.

'Mel? Sweetheart?'

I'd sunk to my knees, my hand still flat on the book. Mum offered me the water bottle she was holding.

'You look quite faint, love. Have a sip of this.'

She pushed the water closer and I went berserk. Flailing out wildly, I dashed the plastic bottle from her hand and sent it rolling over the tiles.

'No!' I screamed. 'No! Get it away from me!'

'Mel, what's the *matter*?'

Mum's face was close, her arms were tight, and though they've told me since that I was screaming, inside my head it didn't sound like proper screams. More like a howling.

Mum kicked my bag away to drop beside me on the floor. 'Mel? Mel!'

At once, the shaking lessened. The awful noises in my ears began to fade. Imogen insisted after that it was only a few seconds at most before my echoing screams turned into sobs. I wouldn't know. The only way that I remember it, there were no sobs at all, just a horrible whining and whimpering, and, as I gradually realized that Mum was holding me and I was safe, the most peculiar leftover feeling of sick unease.

Mum pushed my hair from my face. 'Melly? Are you all right now? Can you walk?'

I shook off the last pricklings of terror.

'I'll be fine. Really.'

Imogen reached for my bag. 'I'll carry this.'

I nodded, and thrust the hateful necklace into her hand. 'Here, take this too.'

'Thanks.'

She rushed ahead to push at the revolving door. Mum kept her arm around me as I stumbled through. And I was glad that Imogen had already spilled out of the doorway into the car park, safely out of hearing, when Mum, still very worried, said to me, 'Mel, that was *terrifying*. You looked positively *haunted*.'

That night, still feeling shaky, I pulled *Wolf!* out of my bag and settled down to it. You don't have to be the greatest reader in the world to know what's coming. It was about a pack of wolves during the summer one of them caught hydrophobia

– a mortal fear of water. Even as I was reading, I could hear echoes of the ghastly howling deep in my head.

'And, *if it's really important,*' Mr Hooper says, '*and you have time, check it a third time.*' So maybe I really should have found some way to get the necklace in my hand again, and touch a photo, to see if, out of nowhere, I suddenly knew something I shouldn't.

But I couldn't face it. For one thing, it was obvious the necklace worked even more fiercely on strangers than on the people who owned it. When I touched *Wolf!*, it had whipped up a storm of a vision. If it had ever worked even one half as vividly for Mrs Tate or Imogen, they would have realized its powers in a flash.

Or . . .

It was the creepiest thought yet. Maybe the necklace recognized its enemies. Maybe it sensed when someone hated it and thought the whole idea of seeing the future was sick and horrible, and quite, quite wrong.

And I *do* think that. I truly do. Suppose I had a necklace like Imogen's, and touched a photo of someone in my family – Dad, say – and suddenly knew that something dreadful was going to happen to him before he came home on his next leave. I couldn't *bear* it. I'd go *mad*.

No, seeing the future is terrible. Crippling. It shouldn't be wished on anyone. And it was hardly Imogen's fault that her dad wasn't around any more, and her mother was the sort who preferred seeing things as 'interesting' or 'fun', to looking at them clearly.

It could be one of Professor Blackstaffe's little problems.

*Someone you know has special
powers that make her life
horribly difficult.*

    Do you:

        *A: Put a stop to it any way you
           can?*

        *B: Not interfere, because it's a 'gift'
           she's been given?*

        *C: Hope things will work out
           right?*

My mother would have been a definite *A*. She had as good as said so.

I wasn't sure if Mrs Tate was *B* or *C*. I did know one thing, though. They were both useless.

So I knew something else, too: it was up to me.

Chapter Fourteen

I had my doubts, though. Lots of people have a gift that makes life hard for them. Dennis has to do two hours on the piano every evening. Clive couldn't come on the French trip because his football coach said it was far too near the county trial. And Moira's parents have to drag her out of bed at five every morning to drive to the ice rink for her solo practice.

At least, though, most of the time, those three enjoy what they're doing. Poor Imogen might be happy enough lost in her daydreams on the little yellow tub in the book corner, but, when I thought about it, the only time I'd ever seen her truly happy was that time in the pool. Who would have thought that taking off a tiny gold chain could cause such a miracle of transformation? Like Snow White in her coffin when the bite of poisoned apple fell from her lips, Imogen had woken to her own real self – lively and noisy, and surrounded by friends (just exactly the sort of person Mr Hooper wishes I was!).

He is a teacher, so I asked him first.

'What is the word for one of those things that makes someone different?'

He looked at me as if I'd spoken to him in Greek. 'What *sort* of thing?'

'Sorry. I can't tell you that.'

'Well, what sort of "different"?'

I glanced at Imogen. 'Sorry. I can't tell you that, either.'

I knew exactly what was coming next.

'All right, Mel. Give me an *example*.'

I didn't want to say a word about gold, or even jewellery. But thinking about the necklace did remind me of the peculiar scratches on the gold. Water and roots, she'd said. So, just for an example, I picked one of those.

'Suppose it was some sort of root.'

'Some sort of *root*?'

It did sound a bit daft. 'All right,' I said hastily. 'Some kind of acorn. A silver acorn that's been lost for years. And, when it's found, everyone who touches it—'

Again, I hesitated. The last thing I wanted was to invite suspicion.

'Everyone who touches it can cook sausages perfectly!'

I'd certainly invited suspicion now.

'Melly,' Mr Hooper asked me, 'do you really think you ought to be in school today? Were you at all feverish this morning?'

I brushed his anxieties aside. 'What is it *called*?' I said. 'I *know* there has to be a word for it. What's it called? A magic something that makes people able to do things they can't do normally.'

'Oh, that!' he said. 'It's called a talisman. Or an amulet. They're both charmed objects. Both have magic powers.'

So it was back to the town library. And now, with the right words, I found my way through all the indexes, and through the lists on screens. And there was loads. A paragraph in this book, a whole chapter in that. Even a few sinister stories. In fact, from reading some, I started to see why these peculiar charmed objects were always being found in places like the darkest caverns and the deepest wells. They'd almost certainly been chucked there by the poor soul who'd had the rotten, miserable luck of being blessed with them before.

Because, all through my reading, one thing was absolutely clear as paint. My first, and worst, suspicion was the right one. For all she might love those magic moments in the book corner, dreaming of playing with puppies, or cantering through moonlight on snow-white steeds, Imogen would never be properly happy until she was rid of the necklace.

I sat in the library window-seat, chewing my nails, working out what to say to her. First, I'd explain about the necklace. Then I'd remind her of all the bad things about the gift, and how it was ruining her school life. And then I'd get her to agree that the best thing to do was—

'Up here? On this shelf? Oh, thank you!'

Over the other side of the tall shelving stacks, someone was speaking to the librarian.

I knew that breathless, eager voice. I peeped round the bookshelves. Yes! It was Imogen's mother. Around her shoulders was a wrap like an old-fashioned counterpane of bright sewn squares, and in her blazing hair were rows and rows of pretty pink plastic slides.

If she'd been my mother, I'd have crawled out of the library with my head in a bag. Instead, I watched her carefully. She drew down book after book, flicking through, peering at indexes in the back and returning them to the bookshelves. And then she settled on a large red book as big as a brick. Pulling a pencil out of the little bag dangling from her wrist, she copied a few words down on a scrap of paper, skipped a few pages, then copied down a few words more.

Then, looking satisfied, she slid the book back on the shelf and left.

I didn't take my eyes off its cover for one single second. So there was no mistake. I pulled the right book out.

And my heart sank. The book in my hand was called *Make More of Magic!*

So it was obvious that, to rescue poor Imogen, I was definitely going to have to get rid of the necklace myself. But how? You can't just snatch a gold chain from around someone's neck and hope they'll not notice. All week, the problem gnawed at me. I tried to slide the idea into her head of taking it off.

'Doesn't it irritate your skin a bit, wearing it all day?' I asked her.

'No,' she said cheerily. 'Mum used to find it scratchy. That's why she hardly ever wore it. But it doesn't bother me in the slightest.'

No hope there, then. So I tried something else. 'Well, don't you worry about losing it when we have sports, or in dancing?'

But she just shook her head. And since the only time I'd ever seen her take it off was at the pool when Mum persuaded her, I was stuck.

And stayed stuck. I couldn't, after all, invite her swimming again, and snaffle it then. Mum would end up in jail. But I was sure there had to be some way of parting Imogen from her necklace.

Twice that week I thought, I'll give up. It's not my problem. And twice, Mr Hooper picked her to fetch the set of reading books, *The Hunted*, out of the cupboard. The first time, she managed to bring them back in a pile balanced on her own workbook and slide them off, untouched, onto his desk. But it did cause an avalanche. So, next day, when he told her to fetch the books again, he added, 'And, this time, Imogen, try carrying them *sensibly*.'

She left her workbook on her desk, and carried the readers in a normal pile. Her hands were shaking, and her eyes were wide with fright.

'Really,' he said, quite sharply. 'All I said to you was "Carry them sensibly". There's no need to look as if I'm going to catch you and put you in the broth pot!'

So that was the ending of yet another book given away – another reading time spoiled. And Imogen didn't look too happy, either, at the ticking off. So I kept thinking, turning crazy, far-fetched plans over and over in my mind as the end of term crept steadily closer.

Imogen kept asking, 'Melly, is something wrong?'

And I'd say, 'Nothing. No. I was just thinking.'

'What about?'

'Nothing.'

And Mr Hooper soon climbed on my back as well.

'Is something worrying you, Mel? Are you getting nervous about the Harries Cup?'

It seemed as good an excuse as any for being too distracted to work properly. So, not exactly lying, I told him in an anxious voice, 'Well, there are only two days, three hours and five minutes before the race . . .'

He put his hand on my shoulder. 'Brace up! You won't have any problems. It's my guess that—'

Imogen swivelled hastily in her seat. 'Mr Hooper! You mustn't *say* that! *Anything* might happen!'

'Yes,' Tasj said, overhearing. 'Melly might get cramp.'

'Or meet a shark under water,' Luke offered helpfully.

'Or get her toe stuck in the pool drain,' suggested Maria.

Mr Hooper let out one of his great who'd-be-a-teacher groans. 'What *is* it about the people in this classroom? Why can't a teacher even have a private word with one of his pupils without everyone in earshot muscling in with their feeble jokes and half-witted suggestions!'

He turned to Imogen, to correct her work. And just as well, because one of those feeble jokes and half-witted suggestions had given me the best idea I'd had – the *only* idea I'd had in a whole week of solid thinking – of how to rescue Imogen and get rid of the necklace without either me or Mum being arrested for robbery.

CHAPTER FIFTEEN

Next morning, I hauled my gym mat onto the pile, and said to Miss Rorty, 'Did you hear about the swimming gala at Green Lane Primary?'

She pulled my mat straighter. 'No. What about it?'

'Tons of things lost,' I told her. 'Watches. Bracelets. Everything.'

'What, *stolen*?'

'No, no,' I assured her. 'Just fallen off in the water.'

'I don't see—'

'To find someone's tiny silver crucifix, they even had to drain the pool.'

'Drain the pool? Really?'

I added the clincher as I turned my back. '*And the school had to pay for it.*'

Her forehead wrinkled. 'Melly, where did you hear—?'

No way of answering that one. And the people behind were pushing. So I fled.

They only pinned up the notice the day before the race.

SWIMMING GALA

*No watches or jewellery
are to be worn tomorrow in
the water. All swimmers are
advised to leave their valuables
at home.*

'I'm just going to tuck my watch into my sock,' I said to Imogen. 'I know it'll be safe.'

'Do you think so?'

'Oh, yes. We're not out of the changing rooms that long. Especially people like you, who are only in the class relay.'

That set her off again, fretting about her one part in the gala – swimming her width.

'Will they mind if I'm the slowest?'

'You won't be slowest,' I assured her. 'Tasj will be slowest. She only learned to swim two weeks ago. And Colin Hamblebury's pretty useless. He just thrashes his arms about and never gets anywhere. And Liz doesn't put herself out much. So you'll probably even be faster than her.'

Imogen was still looking worried. 'You really do believe you have it taped, this swimming gala, don't you, Mel?'

'You bet,' I said, not mentioning that, this year, it was going to be more important than ever to judge it right. I'd worked out that I'd only have eight or so seconds' leeway before Toby Harrison would come steaming up behind, with Surina behind him, and at least one of the Trent twins after her. One clumsy dive, and I'd lose most of my head start. So I had two more things to practise now, and only one session in the pool to get both of them perfect before the big race.

'Nervous?' asked Imogen, but I wouldn't say. For one thing, although she only had one measly width to swim, each time I caught her eye, it seemed to me that she was still staring at me anxiously, and I didn't want to make her worse. And for another, she was the last person in the world I could confide in this time, because my plan to win the Harries Cup now included wasting six seconds getting rid of her necklace.

Six seconds exactly. I'd timed it. My new 'touch-the-bottom' tumble turn took four seconds longer than usual. And then you had to add on another two before I was back up to speed. It was still a dead cert, if not the romp home I'd wanted. But there seemed no way out. No point in explaining to anyone about the necklace if no-one was going to be tough enough to throw it away for good. For that was the only thing. All the books said so.

I could try and explain to her mother. The problem was, I wasn't sure what Mrs Tate would do. My mother would have taken a ferry out to sea, to drop the pesky thing deeper. But Mrs Tate was different. You only had to peek in her enchanted back garden with its secret dells and perky elves, or join in eating iced fairy cakes in one of her story-book tea times, to know she didn't really live in the sensible grown-up world where people look after their children properly and protect them from things that might damage them. Look how excited she already was about Imogen's weird powers – 'Anything "special" happen?' If I explained that I'd worked out that they came through the gold chain, instead of wanting to hurl it over a cliff into the sea, she'd more than likely clap her hands together and tell us it was *exactly* like something in one of her favourite old books, *Ellen's Enchanted Necklace*. She'd look up 'amulets' in *Make More of Magic!*, and want Imogen to keep it to see what would happen.

If Imogen ended up looking grey and haunted enough under the strain, then Mrs Tate might finally come to her senses and lock the chain safely away for a while. But not for long, I'd bet. After a bit, the memory of how it had chewed up her daughter's life would begin to fade round the edges. She'd soon forget how rotten Imogen's schoolwork had been, and how people used to move away when she came near, and how she could scarcely bear to touch some books, and day-dreamed her life away when she picked up others.

And, one rainy day, out it would come again. 'Just in case you're a bit better at it, now that you're older,' or, 'Just in case, this time, it only tells you about *nice* things.'

But I'm not tired and distracted. And I can open any book I like without jumping for fright, or acting as if the pages have scorched me. And, over the week, I had been reading up on all sorts of magic rings and lamps and mirrors and swords and boots and wands and crystals, and even pebbles. I'd found a dozen stories called things like *The Amulet in the Wood*, and *The Silver Talisman,* and *Sasha's Charmed Bracelet*, and *The Enchanted Cap of Gold*.

And I'd learned this. You weren't free till you threw whichever horrible thing it was away.

As far as possible. Firmly. For good, for sure, and for *ever*.

CHAPTER SIXTEEN

So I said nothing. Nothing to Mum, when she made me my favourite pancakes for breakfast – 'to stoke me up properly'. Nothing to Dad, who must have put his alarm on in the middle of the night to phone and wish me luck from Singapore. And nothing when people looked up as I walked in the classroom, and asked, 'Are you nervous, Mel?' or, 'Getting excited?'

'A bit,' was all I answered, as if the Harries Cup was the one thing on my mind, not jewellery theft, and spoiling a perfectly good friendship. And I kept my cool front up all through the morning, and all through lunch, and on the walk to the pool. When Miss Rorty winked at me during the Grand Opening, I winked back. I tried not to worry as I inspected Councillor Archibald Leroy for signs of a possible heart attack. And when we were sent off to change, straight after the fourth years, I made as many jokey faces as everyone else while Miss Rankin prowled round the cubicles, fussing and scolding.

'Hurry up. There are still loads of people to come through these changing rooms. Don't leave so much as a sock in the cubicles. Put your stuff neatly on the benches.'

Her eyes fell on Imogen's pile. 'And *sensibly*, please, Imogen.'

I could see why she'd said it. Imogen had rolled up her uniform into a giant sausage. Clearly, she'd taken my advice and hidden the necklace inside it. But even without looking, I would have known she wasn't wearing it, because the first thing Miss Rankin did as she scolded was drop both hands cheerfully onto her shoulders to push her back to her clothes pile. And only a moment later, Maria slid an arm in hers. 'Hey, Immy. Ready to break the world water speed record?'

Imogen turned to me. 'Coming?'

I nodded, and, as a trio, we splashed through the footbath into the brightness of the pool and huddled round one of the radiators, waiting for Mrs Parkin to get round to calling out our first big race.

It wasn't long.

'Inter-Class Relay! Mr Hooper's, Mrs Potter's and Ms Robinson's classes. Half of you on each side, please. One width each!'

Our class always puts the weedy swimmers on first, to get them over. Tasj started us off, and she was absolutely useless, as usual. Then Colin Hamblebury fell in and thrashed his arms about a bit, losing us half a width more. And Liz hadn't improved much. She just stroked her way across idly, not even bothering to glance to the side to see how the other two classes were doing.

But Imogen did brilliantly. She ended up swimming against Norman Pizarro and Tara Bloor, neither of whom are much good. But still she made up miles in her short width, and when she got out of the water, everyone was cheering.

'Well done, Immy!'

'Excellent swim, Miss Mermaid!'

She looked delighted. And I was really pleased
as well, because it showed that what I had in
mind was right. It couldn't have been more than
a few minutes since she'd taken off the necklace,
and look! Already she seemed to have melted in
and become just like one of the others. She was
laughing and joking, and huddling round the
radiator as if she were just one more companion-
able bee in a hive. They'll be plaiting her hair
next, I remember thinking. And, just for a
moment, I wondered if I would be jealous when it

was all over, and she was in a gang with them, and no longer a loner like I am.

And, no, I thought. I really don't think that I'll give a hoot. It seems to me that you can only get truly jealous of people if they are somehow exactly the way you've always wanted to be (or think you are already, but others don't realize).

But I don't want to be what Mr Hooper calls, 'a little more gregarious'.

I just want to be me.

And Imogen should have the right to be her real self, too. So seeing her leaning back against the radiator, laughing, with the wet ends of her hair being flicked by Hal, made it easier to sneak away, back through the footbaths into the crowded changing rooms, where even Miss Rankin had lost track of who was coming and going.

'Excuse me . . . Can I get through please? . . . Sorry . . .' Finally I made it past the busy cubicles back to the bench. I glanced round quickly, then slid my fingers inside Imogen's tightly wrapped pile of clothes. And all I can say is that I hope she makes a better job of hiding the next piece of jewellery somebody gives her.

The glittering loops of this one practically fell into my hand.

And it was the weirdest thing. Suddenly I felt

as if I were already underwater – way, way down, lost in a storm of bubbles.

'Oh!'

I clawed at my throat. I couldn't breathe and my knees were buckling beneath me.

'Are you all right?' A little second year had heard me gasping. 'Shall I go and get Miss Rankin for you?'

I was so close to fainting that I dropped the necklace, which fell in a fold of towel. Only then did I manage to gather my senses.

'No, no. I'm fine,' I said, even before the wave of panic passed, leaving me even more sure I had to get this horrid chain of Imogen's out of our lives. Not even caring whose towel it was I was borrowing, I scrunched the necklace up in it as tightly as I could without touching, and pushed my way through all the second years rushing out of the cubicles, to hurry back the way I'd come, towards the footbaths.

And how I thought I might intimidate a golden chain with my determination, I'll never know. (I'm not in the habit of talking to jewellery.) But as I splashed through the arch, I found myself whispering to it, horribly fiercely:

'Don't think you're going to beat *me*. Because you're *not*!'

I heard a voice behind me. 'Keep your hair on, Mel. Only a race.'

I spun round. Stepping out of the footbaths on the boys' side was Toby Harrison, who'd win the Harries Cup for sure if I weren't swimming.

'I didn't mean you,' I said hastily.

He looked offended. 'I'm sure I don't know who you *do* mean, then.'

How can you try and explain you're talking to a necklace? You can't. So I shut up, except to say, 'Well, good luck, anyway.'

He grinned. 'And good luck to you, Melly. See you at the finish – when I look back over my shoulder!'

'Keep dreaming, Toby!'

He went off towards his friends, and I stuffed the towel under the heating pipe, and hurried back to join our relay queue. It had become so short that people were panicking.

'Mel, where have you *been?*'

'We thought you'd *vanished.*'

'We still have nearly half a width to make up. You can do it, can't you?'

Can I save half a width? Can Granny knit? I did the fastest racing dive Miss Rorty says she's ever seen in a school gala. I was across the pool so fast that poor Hugh Gregory had no idea his class had lost till he shook the hair from his eyes and saw my fingertips already on the ledge, and me turning, laughing.

'But I was—'

I didn't hear the end for cheers.
'Brilliant, Mel!'
'*Saved!*'
I did a celebratory backwards flip in the water.
I thought I might as well. I knew I wasn't going
to beat any speed records winning the Cup race –

not with the tumble turn that I'd been practising up at the deep end. As soon as Miss Rorty saw that, she'd stop all her cheery nodding and waving. She'd be too busy wondering what on earth could have happened to turn a race that should have been a dead cert from the very start into a risky business with only three seconds to spare.

But there was no way round it. And I would at least still win the Cup. In my last practice session I'd timed it over and over. Four extra seconds for the tumble turn, and two more to get up to speed.

It could be done. And I'd do it.

And the best thing was that I couldn't possibly be tempted to fiddle with the plan. How could I? It was all worked out. Only one way to do it. Start from the shallower end, and, in a three-length race, you only get one tumble turn under the boards.

Or – put it another way – only one chance.

CHAPTER SEVENTEEN

Miss Rorty held the whistle between her teeth and looked down the line. Eight of us on our starting blocks. And me already shivering because, to get the right one, I'd had to take my place ages before.

'Ready?'

She raised an eyebrow because I wasn't in my usual stance. But finally, after about a billion years, she blew the whistle.

I lost the first two seconds then and there.

You try it. Try a racing dive, flinging yourself out over the water, stretching so thin you cut air. Then try it with one hand clamped to your hip to stop a slinky, cunning gold chain wriggling out of your swimsuit and landing on the tiles to shriek '*Stolen!*' at everyone and shame you for ever.

You'd have played safe like I did, and done a bellyflop too.

But in the huge, embarrassing splash of it, I did at least manage to hook out the chain. I couldn't do my usual strong spading through the water with it grasped in my hand. So it took time even to pull ahead of four particular pairs of feet I've never seen in front of me in my life, and reach the deep end. By then, at least, I'd even managed to pass the slower of the twins. But Toby and Surina were well ahead. And even Josh Murphy was thundering along at a good pace.

But I still had to do my stupid tumble turn. It might sound mad, but what was mostly in my mind was the thought of poor Miss Rorty who'd spent so much time training and encouraging me, and knew how important this race had become, and how much I wanted to win it. I knew she'd be standing at the edge, filled with dismay, wondering what on earth had happened to her best swimmer. First, that dreadfully clumsy starting dive; then the ham-fisted way I was ploughing through the water with one hand firmly clenched. And, now, coming up, the worst tumble turn she could imagine.

But there was no way round it. Instead of tucking up my legs and twisting fast to kick off straight and hard the way I'd come, I was about to waste even more time swimming down to the bottom.

To drop the necklace down the drain, where it would lie till, in the next water change, it would be swept into the sewers and out to sea.

Out of our lives for ever. Just like in the books.

And now the pool end was within my reach. Gathering myself into a ball, I tumbled perfectly, as I've been taught, and practised for so many hours. And, though it sounds crazy, even as I was doing it, I felt the necklace stir in my hand as if . . .

I have to say it. As if it *knew*.

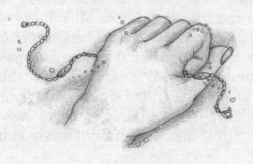

And then the battle started. All round me there blew up that storm of bubbles I'd sensed before. At first, I thought they must be mine. I thought I must be letting out my breath – too fast, too soon.

But it was nothing to do with me. It was the necklace. Even in all that cool water, the thing was scalding my fingers. Twisting and burning, trying to distract me, trying to make me let it go – *anything* rather than let itself be fed through one of the tiny squares of the drain grille and dropped out of sight for ever. That spiteful little chain of gold put up the worst fight. The water churned so fiercely I could barely see. My right hand burned so badly that, if I'd had breath to spare, I would have yelped.

But I was suddenly furious. It was so *unfair*. I'd trained for months to win the Harries Cup. I didn't ask Imogen Tate to come to our school. I didn't ask Mr Hooper to put her next to me – in fact I as good as begged him *not* to!

And just because I'd tried to fit in with what everyone wanted – be friendly, not hide in my books, get interested in real life for a change – everything had gone sour. And even swimming, the only other thing I liked and was good at, was being spoiled.

You can't talk under water. You lose your air in

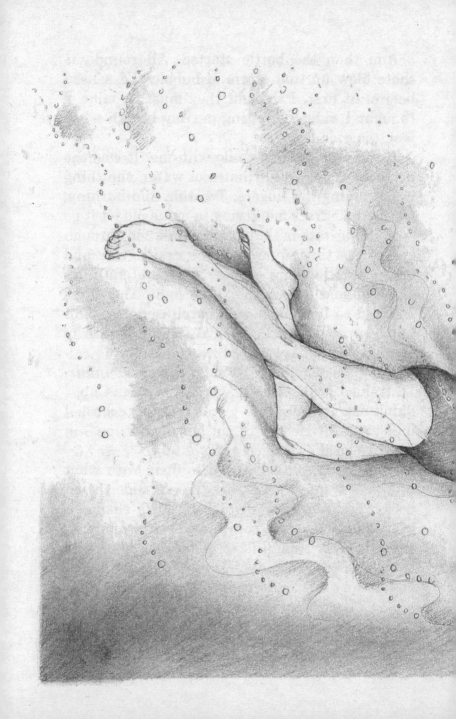

one large, glistening flood of bubbles. But if I could, I would have said it over again to Imogen's horrible necklace.

'Don't think you're going to beat *me*. Because you *won't*!'

Instead, I put my energy into one last enormous pull through the water. Clutching the chain, I swam down through the blizzard of angry bubbles till there, at last, I saw the drain.

And slammed my hand down flat. I didn't trust the necklace not to wriggle off. I rubbed the links of it over the grille till suddenly I felt the coils vanishing beneath my fingers as it went down. Now, under the flat of my palm, I could feel nothing but the clasp, a hard metallic lump still stubbornly clinging to the grille edge. And that's when I had to make the worst decision of my life.

'Come on!' I tried to tell myself. 'That's it. You've done it. Swim back up, quick. There's still a chance. You could still do it. You could still win the Harries Cup.'

But that old clasp was hanging on. And I knew why. Oh, I'd swim off, thinking I'd done the job and Imogen was safe. But the necklace would beat me. The clasp would cling on to the grille till evening session – Intermediate Diving. One after another for an hour, Miss Pollard's pupils would be plunging down. Someone was bound to spot it. I could hear them now.

'Miss Pollard! Miss Pollard! Look what I've found trapped in the drain. It must belong to someone in the gala.'

She'd reach down to take it. 'It looks quite valuable. I'd better drop it by the school tomorrow.'

No need to guess the rest. By break time, it would be back round Imogen's neck, strangling her life.

Professor Blackstaffe would have put it plainly enough.

To do something seriously important for a friend, you have to make a sacrifice.
> *Do you:*
>> *A: Do it?*
>> *B: Kid yourself your thing matters just as much?*

A cup's a cup. It might be made to matter in a book. But it's not serious. Not like real life.

So I just did it – used up my very last spare second or two prising that hateful, stubborn little clasp off the drain grille, and pushing it through. I'd run out of air. My lungs were on fire. But I still stayed to watch it sink – down, down, resentfully, till it was out of sight.

And then, at last, I let myself push away, up like an arrow. Breaking the surface, I took the very deepest breath, and stormed off after the others. I don't think I've ever in my life swum any faster. I pounded along, meeting the others coming back the other way for their third and last length.

I turned just as Surina reached the half-way mark. It was a brilliant tumble – fast and strong.

I knew at least Miss Rorty would be pleased to see I hadn't let her training down in front of everyone. It was my best turn ever.

I slid through the water like a needle through silk. First I saw Surina's toes, and then her knees, and then, since she was tiring, with one last great heave, I spun ahead. I took my next breath on the other side, to check the enemy. And, to my surprise, saw I'd left the other twin behind as well, and one more pull would bring me up to Toby.

I'm a machine in water when I'm pounding hard. Miss Rorty says it's like watching pistons in the engine of a great ship, or valves in a power station. I pulled on and on. And if the Harries Cup had only been a race one metre longer, there is not a shred of doubt I would have won it.

As it was, I lost.

CHAPTER EIGHTEEN

They were all there for me, I'll give them that. Miss Rorty wrapped a towel round me so fast that only she and I knew when she pressed the corner of it to my face, she wasn't blotting my hair at all, only stemming my tears of rage and frustration.

Toby didn't crow. All he said was, 'Jeez, that was close! Just two more seconds, Mel, and you'd have done it.'

Mr Hooper came up and hugged me even before he shook Toby's hand. Then he grinned ruefully. 'Oh, blimey. Now we're going to have to exhume poor Mrs Harries so she can change the age rules on her Cup race.'

And Maria said she saw Councillor Leroy whispering to his wife before she slipped out for a moment. And that it wasn't just a mistake that the brand new award – Best Overall Swimmer – had been left off the programme. She says the pool keeps fat round medals like the one he gave to me behind the counter as spares in case of dead heats in competitions.

So I knew what they all thought. And it was comforting. But not the same, even if everyone was cheering and stamping and giving me the thumbs up all the way back to the changing rooms. Because it was the Cup I wanted. And Mr Hooper can joke about digging up Mrs Harries all he likes, but it's over now. Finished. No prize is the same if the people who organize it have to change the rules so you can win it. Who wants that?

But it was worth it, I suppose – not that you'd think it from the way Imogen turned on me in the changing rooms.

First, she was just a bit panicked.

'My necklace! Where's it *gone*?'

'Isn't it there?'

'No!' She rooted through her clothes pile in a frenzy, tossing and shaking everything. 'It's *vanished*.'

She looked up wildly. All around us, people were gathering up their piles of clothes and making for the cubicles.

'Please!' she called. 'Everyone look for my necklace. It's disappeared.'

Maria was in there like a flash, of course. 'Miss Rorty said we weren't to—'

'I know what Miss Rorty said!' Imogen snapped. 'I *know*. I have *ears*. But *Melly* said—'

She broke off and turned to look at me. You could see the first glimmer of suspicion. 'Mel said she was quite sure it would be safe . . .'

I had to try and pretend I cared. 'What's *that* supposed to mean?'

'You know.'

'No,' I said. 'I'm afraid I don't.' I turned my back on her. I think I was really rather hoping she'd back off and leave me alone after my disappointment. But I was wrong.

'You *must* know, Melly.'

I tried to sound outraged. 'Me? Why *me*?'

'Be*cause*,' she hissed, 'you were the only one who knew my necklace was wrapped up in there.' Her eyes narrowed. 'In fact,' she added, 'now I come to think, you were the one who suggested I left it there in the first place.'

That's when I panicked a little. 'What would I want with your stupid necklace?'

Her eyes flashed. Her voice rose. 'You tell me, Mel! All I know is, you've taken an interest in it from the start. Practically the first thing you ever said to me was how much you liked it. *And* you asked if it was precious, and said you didn't think you'd ever be given anything that valuable yourself.'

Mirrors run all the way along the wall above the benches. Even the people with their backs to us could see I was blushing. The whole, huge, echoing changing room had fallen quiet.

Except for us.

'You really think I took it?'

She stared deep in my eyes. 'Yes,' she said. 'Yes, I do. In fact, I'm sure you did. I think you've hidden it somewhere and you'll sneak back for it later. And I think that's why you lost your stupid, *stupid* race, Mel. Because you were too busy planning to steal my necklace – or too guilty after doing it – to swim your fastest.'

And wasn't I tempted, then, to spoil everything I'd done to save her from her horrible necklace! 'I haven't got it!' I could have said to her. 'But I will tell you that while I was swimming in my stupid,

stupid race, I did see something glittery lying at the bottom of the pool, right by the drain.'

That would have fixed her. They'd have found it and given it back to her in no time.

And I was tempted. Very, very tempted. But I just gritted my teeth and thought of what Professor Blackstaffe would have said if he had overheard me. And at least I was sure now that I hadn't thrown away the Cup for nothing. She'd *never* find the necklace. She just doesn't read enough. If she read books, she'd understand that people live their *own* lives – lives completely special to them. They have their own things that matter, their own ways of going about them, and their own words to talk about them if they want. They don't go through their lives like plastic counters moving round a board game, each one a bit different on the surface so you can tell them apart, but all the same inside. I wanted to shake her. 'Look at me!' I wanted to shout. 'Look at me! Hello! It's *Mel* here, speaking. *Mel!* You know! This person you've sat next to for five whole weeks, and call a friend. This person who's spent *three whole years* wanting to win a race. Do you really think I'd toss the whole lot over just to take the chance to snatch a stupid necklace I wouldn't even be able to wear? *Do* you? *Do* you?'

But what was the point in setting Imogen off

thinking? Pushed, she might just work out why someone like me might *really* want to take her necklace.

Then she'd be one step nearer to working out where it was.

No. At least till the pool had been drained, it was best to say nothing.

CHAPTER NINETEEN

But everyone else talked. Toby Harrison set it all off by accident, mentioning we'd wished one another good luck coming out of the footbaths.

'So maybe Imogen's right,' someone as gossipy as Maria must have said. 'After all, what was she doing back there again ten minutes later?'

And tongues began to wag. People remembered that I'd disappeared till almost the end of the relay. And then the little girl whose towel I'd borrowed without asking popped up to mention she'd found it hidden under the hot water pipes. Had Imogen looked for her necklace there?

And that's when Mr Hooper got involved.

'So, Mel,' he said, coming up behind me after next morning's Assembly. 'Time for a little chat?'

'I suppose so.'

He didn't take me to the classroom. Instead, he dropped a hand on my shoulder and steered me down to the quiet end of the corridor. Then he leaned back against the door.

'About this necklace that Imogen shouldn't even have been wearing in the first place . . .' was how he began.

At least that made it easier for me to lift my head.

'I know how it looks,' I said. 'And I know what she's been saying. But, honestly, I never wanted it and I haven't got it.'

No lies in that, so it came out sounding the truth, and he believed it.

'So what were you doing back in the changing rooms?'

'I was so nervous that I . . . I needed to . . .' Again, I stopped, and he assumed I was too embarrassed to finish the sentence.

'And what about little Fay Tucker's towel?'

'That was me,' I confessed. 'I was frozen. I was shivering all over. I saw it lying there, and I know it was wrong, but, with the big race coming up, I thought . . .'

'You thought it was important and, if she knew, she wouldn't mind?'

He hadn't said *what* I thought was important. So what he'd said was true, in its own way.

'That sort of thing.'

He eyed me steadily. 'Well, Mel,' he said. 'I've known you ever since you were in first year and, as far as I know, you've never snitched so much as a Snoopy rubber from anyone – except from under their nose to start a fight. So I'm going to choose to believe you.'

'I expect you'll be the only one,' I couldn't help saying.

He shrugged. 'I'm not so sure about that.' And then he grinned. 'Now if it had been a *book* she'd accused you of pinching . . . But a *necklace*. Oh, I'm not so sure about that.'

And I did suddenly feel a little hope. That's true, I thought. I've been here years and years, and they all know me. But Imogen has only been here for a matter of weeks, and they're so used to thinking she's a little strange, it might turn out quite easy for them to just assume she's wrong as well.

And that's exactly how it all worked out. Maria told me, after. 'As soon as Mr Hooper had made that excuse to send you off to the staffroom with those keys, he started on at us about how very unlikely it was that someone who'd never even bothered to wear rings or bracelets or anything, would care two hoots about a silly necklace.'

'Did he say "silly"? Did he really?'

'Well, no. But you could sort of hear it in his voice. And Imogen was furious, you could tell, as if, just because she and her mother think you stole her precious necklace, we all have to think that too. She sat there with a stony look. And, after, she said that she was going to ask her mum if she could go back to her old school.'

'Really?'

'That's right. She says that after the gala she bumped into several of her old classmates, and they were really nice to her. And *they* believe her.'

'So she's going back next term?'

'No. Sooner than that. Next week, she hopes. She doesn't even want to come back to us tomorrow.'

'Leaving so soon!'

It just popped out, because there was one last thing I had to do. Edging past Maria, I pelted off to the book corner. On the top shelf, crammed in between *The Bumper Book of Ghost Stories* and *Weird Tales II*, was *Lucy Fainlight*.

It looks like nothing as a book. The picture on the cover is just a girl in a crinoline skirt. She looks quite drippy, as if nothing of any interest could ever happen to her. The book's so old, it has that tiny print everyone hates reading because it takes for ever to get down a page. The paragraphs go on for *days*, and there are only three pictures, and they're all hidden behind tissue. Probably the only reason it's still on the shelf is because it was donated by Mrs Trent's own granny.

But it's the creepiest book I've ever read. It's terrifying. Horrible. From the first page, your skin starts crawling. I'm not even going to begin to tell you what happens to poor Lucy Fainlight. But it's a ghastly story.

"Again she heard it!"

Outside the classroom, I bumped into Toby.

'Do me a favour,' I begged him. 'Give this book to Imogen.'

He gave me a funny look. 'The buzzer's gone. Aren't you coming in?'

'Not right this minute.'

Shrugging, he took the book. On his way over to his place by the window, he dropped it in front of Imogen.

'Here,' he said. 'Present from Melly.'

I thought that might be a mistake. She might ignore it. But, no. Clearly curious, she glanced at it, then, gingerly as usual, reached out to turn it over so she could see the picture on the front. I stood in the doorway, watching and waiting as her fingers touched the cover.

And nothing happened. Not a thing. No draining face. No trembling fingertips. No growing look of dismay. She might as well have been inspecting a cauliflower for all the emotion she displayed.

That's when I knew I'd done it. The girl who only had to lean back against a photo on a wall to know exactly who was going to win the Harries Cup now didn't even have the first inklings of a clue what horrors lay in store for Lucy Fainlight. Now she was free. Free from pretending she didn't know things that she did. Free from half-lies and horrible decisions (like having to let me worry about nice Mr Leroy because she couldn't bring herself to tell me that it wasn't that he wouldn't be on the podium to hand me the Cup. It was that I wouldn't be there to take it!).

And free to have surprises. Read books without knowing the end. Go back to her old school and be delighted at just how quickly and easily she could make friends. She would be happy, the miseries of the future no longer dripping like poisonous rain into the days of here and now, spoiling her life.

She would be free.

And so would I. I could barely believe it. Free to sneak off and read, just like before. Free to hide back in books. Free from the shackles of having to sit by someone at lunch, and on trips, and before Assembly.

Free to unplug from the chatter and blot them all out, as usual. Free to be *me*.

It only took Mr Hooper half a day to suss me out.

'Melly, you have the most seraphic smile on your face. Go on. Admit it. You're delighted to have this desk beside you back empty.'

He raised the lid, and saw that I'd colonized it already with half the new stock from the library.

He raised his eyebrows at me.

'It's only sensible,' I told him. 'It's only if you've read them that you know exactly which section you should put them in.'

'Oh, I see,' he said. 'It's not just that you're planning a long and pleasant convalescence from the strain of having a friend for a few days.'

I showed my outrage. 'She was here *six whole weeks*.'

He shook his head. 'Oh, Melly, Melly. I've said it before. What on earth are we going to do with you?'

'Nothing,' I told him firmly. 'Just don't fret. I've *told* you. I've told *everyone*. I'm happy reading. I prefer the company of books.'

'You really won't miss her, will you?'

'No,' I said. 'I really won't.'

And it is true. I'm not sorry that she's gone. I wish her well. I hope her mum gets over the disappointment. I have felt a tiny bit uneasy once or twice, mostly because it was meddling. But if I had to face the same choice over again, I'd still pick *A*, even if Professor Blackstaffe were standing there scowling. I'd still do exactly what I did.

So, truthfully, I only have one real regret. And that's that, the very first time I came across something in real life halfway as exciting as something in a story, I was the one who put a stop to it. I was the one who, when you think about it, closed it up.

I'd never have done that with a book. But there again, as I explained right at the start, that's just the way I am. Though I've gone to the trouble of writing this book for you, the fact is that I have *always* preferred reading.

A Note from the Author

What is the difference between a good reader and a real bookworm?

One of the questions children often ask authors is, 'Do you put yourself in your books?' I confess that, in *Bad Dreams*, I have written the closest account of myself as a child.

I was like Mel. I thought the same way she does. I had the same passion for reading and the same habit of trying to get to all the good books first. I hoarded books and comics everywhere so there would always, *always* be something to read.

I'm not sure how people turn into bookworms. I should think it's probably partly genetic – like happening to have blue eyes or brown hair – and partly being lucky enough to meet the right books at the right time. You're blessed if your parents and teachers know the value of libraries and second-hand bookshops, and make the effort to see you have a constant supply of fresh things to read.

But most of it comes from inside you. There are those who secretly believe (as Mel tries to explain to her teacher) that books are in some ways far more real than real life itself. They can certainly bring as much pleasure. (The American humourist, Logan Pearsall Smith, is famous for once declaring, 'People say Life is the thing, but I much prefer reading.')

I learned to read when I was very young indeed. When I was three, my mother had triplet babies and, to make things a little easier, I was sent straight to the next door infant school. Nobody explained that I was really only there to be babysat, and didn't need to try to keep up with the rest. So by the age of four I was a very good reader. Then, when the primary school insisted I wouldn't be old enough to join them for another year, my lovely infant school headteacher gave me the run of the glass-fronted bookshelf in her office, I still remember tapping nervously on the door, being beckoned inside, and sitting quietly on her carpet choosing my next few books, then trying to stop the glass doors juddering horribly along their wooden runnels when it was time to slide them closed again.

A whole school year, at seven, with nothing to do but sit and read. Some people would have hated it. I was in seventh heaven. I've *always* preferred reading. When I was young, my mother was forever trying to shoo me out of the house. 'It's such a nice day. Why don't you go outside?'

I always tried to wriggle out of it, preferring to stay inside and read about someone else in a story who had done just that.

And find out what happened to them . . .

Anne Fine

anne Fine

Frozen Billy

Could a stage dummy possibly have the
power to destroy a family?

Frozen Billy is Uncle Len's ventriloquist's dummy.
Clarrie knows he's not real.
But then her brother Will joins in the music-hall act.
And suddenly – creepily – everything begins
to go horribly wrong . . .

'Superb' THE TIMES

'A riveting tale with sinister undertones'
BOOKS FOR KEEPS

'Full of terrific characters and deceptions
and intrigues' TES

'Fine's genius for storytelling reaches new heights:
simple, direct, and with a subtle period feel to
narrative and dialogue' INDEPENDENT

0 440 86630 8

www.kidsatrandomhouse.co.uk

The More the Merrier

Three days of family fun?

Cousin Titania is writing soppy notes to Santa.
Uncle Tristram is chucking potatoes at the cat.
And Mum is on the verge of a breakdown.
Ralph is not having a good Christmas . . .

'A wickedly seasonal tale' *THE TIMES*

'Anne Fine at her wittiest' *TES*

'There's a grim cast in this hilarious but barbed
story of how Christmas can go so wrong for
so many people' *GUARDIAN*

0 440 86733 9

www.kidsatrandomhouse.co.uk